POMEGRANATES for PEACE

POMEGRANATES for PEACE

MIRIAM HALAHMY

WHERE STORIES BEGIN

First published in the UK in 2025 by ZunTold
www.zuntold.com

Text copyright © Miriam Halahmy 2025
Cover design by Isla Bousfield-Donohoe

The moral right of the author has been asserted.
All rights reserved.
Unauthorised duplication contravenes existing laws.

A catalogue record for this book is available
from the British Library

ISBN 978-1-915758-30-9
1 3 5 7 9 10 8 6 4 2

Printed and bound by Interak, Poland.

This book is dedicated to Peace in the Middle East

All the world is a very narrow bridge —
but the essential thing is to never be afraid.
                    – *Nachman of Bratislav*

AUTHOR'S FOREWORD

The inspiration behind this book has been my personal commitment to working for Peace over many decades and the dozens of grassroots organisations in Israel committed to building Peace in the Middle East, even during the most difficult times.

My book is set a few weeks after October 7th, 2023, when Hamas, the organisation which governs Gaza, launched an attack on Israel. Thousands of people – Israeli Jews, Muslims, Christians, Arabs, Bedouin, foreign workers and foreign students – were killed and injured. Many people were taken hostage into Gaza and hidden away. A war started between Israel and Gaza which resulted in a terrible loss of life and great suffering of ordinary civilians on both sides.

As a result of the Israel/Gaza war, divisions opened

up in our communities in the UK, America and all over the world. In our schools, the atmosphere between Jewish and non-Jewish students was sometimes very unpleasant.

As a children's author and former teacher, I decided to write a book for young people to open the discussion. As a Peace Activist, I have run groups with Jews and Muslims, Israelis and Palestinians, to create a bridge across our divided communities. I have also run Peace Workshops in a lycée in France as part of the Erasmus Programme, bringing students together from different countries to learn about each other. This included both Muslim and Jewish students.

I believe that all divided communities can build bridges and find ways to come together, despite the pain and suffering inflicted by both sides. I hope that my book will inspire young people from all backgrounds to work for the kind of future they wish to build.

Shalom. Salaam. Peace to all Life on Earth.

Miriam Halahmy
London, UK
January 2025

1
Tamara's Cousin

November 2023

Tamara arrived at the school gates before her friends. It was a cold, grey Tuesday morning in November. Fallen leaves were heaped in wet piles on the streets, and she'd nearly skidded over as she strode to school, hands in pockets, insides churning with anger.

Standing by the gates, she was quite glad to be alone. Her life was about to change forever, and her famous hot temper was threatening to burst out at any moment.

Tamara reached inside her school sweater to feel the gold chain and Star of David Gran had given to her two years ago, on her tenth birthday.

"I'll never take it off," she'd declared, as Gran had fastened the Star around her neck.

They weren't allowed to wear jewellery in school,

so Tamara always kept her necklace hidden and tucked it away in her school shoes for PE.

But even touching her beautiful Star couldn't keep her calm today. Dad called Tamara's temper red hot like chillis. That temper was always getting her into trouble and now, in Abbey Park High School, with so many new teachers and new things to learn, Tamara felt on the edge of an outburst several times a day.

The eldest and also tallest girl in Year 7, Tamara had turned twelve on their very first day, a few weeks back in September. Generous, loyal and always up for a challenge, Tamara made friends easily, despite her temper, which other kids found funny. Abbey Park High School was in North London, with many different nationalities and a group of Jewish kids in each year. Tamara's mum had wanted Tamara to go to a Jewish high school. But Tamara had refused to be separated from her absolute best and forever friend Yaz, let alone Arthur and Josh. They'd all four been friends since primary school.

As Tamara scrolled down her phone now, eyebrows furrowed, insides clenched, a voice broke into her thoughts.

"Hey, Tam."

It was Yaz.

Tamara threw her arms around her friend and gave her a tight hug.

"Whoa," said Yaz, pulling back, her face split in a grin. "What's up?"

Before Tamara could answer, Arthur came over, football under his arm as if it was an extra limb. Arthur was rarely seen without a football. He was not only the best striker in the Year 7 team, but he'd recently been taken into the school's Under-15 team and had already scored in their first match. Arthur had reached hero status. "But they're all bigger than you," Yaz had said with a shudder when they'd stayed behind to watch a game.

"So what?" Arthur had said with a smile. "I'm faster than anyone."

"And more skilled," Josh had said. Now, Josh came to join the other three and Tamara felt some of the turmoil inside her begin to settle, as her friends bunched round.

"What's happened?" said Yaz in her quiet voice.

Tamara stared at her friend, Yazmin Amina Ali, with her light brown skin and long, straight hair, which Tamara had always envied. Tamara's hair, darker than Yaz's, was so frizzy and bushy. It was impossible to straighten and she wore it much shorter than her friend. Yaz's family were from Pakistan, but her mum and dad had grown up in London. They went to mosque sometimes, like Tamara's family went to shul sometimes, but neither family was very religious. They all lived in the same semi-circle close. The two families had moved into their houses during the same week when Yazmin and Tamara were babies, and they'd all become firm friends.

Yaz was the calm, logical one. The one who could stop Tamara from going chilli mad with the pressure of her cool hand on an arm.

Tamara's voice was beginning to shake now as she said, "My cousin Gidi is coming over from Israel tomorrow to stay with us. He's having my bedroom."

"Why's he giddy?" asked Arthur, giving his ball a couple of bounces.

Arthur was a bit shorter than Tamara but with long muscular legs. He kept his hair short and had a determined line to his chin. His skin was more golden brown than Yaz's. Arthur's family were from Thailand, although there was only his mum since he was little. Arthur could move as fast as Tamara's temper on the football pitch, and he never lost his cool. "I'm going to get into the Premier League and buy my mum a house," Arthur was always telling them.

Josh's dad was Jewish and although his mum wasn't, Josh knew quite a bit about Israel. Now he said, grinning at Tamara, "She doesn't mean giddy like that. It's an Israeli name."

"His name's Gideon," said Tamara in an impatient voice. "Gidi for short, spelt G-I-D-I."

"So, what's the problem?" said Arthur,

Tamara opened her mouth to let out the hot rush of chilli words bubbling up inside her and then shut her mouth again.

Yaz gave her a surprised look.

Tamara looked down at her screen, hands trembling.

I can't say anything, she thought. They won't understand if I tell them what I did last night.

An even worse thought came to her. They might not want to be friends anymore if they find out.

She had to fight to hold back tears.

Arthur and Josh had started to tap the football between them. Yaz was checking her phone too. They seemed to sense that Tamara needed time to push down her anger about something.

Last night was still so fresh and painful in Tamara's mind. If she was honest, things hadn't been good at home for a while.

Ever since the terrible attack on Israel on October 7th, just a few weeks ago, it felt as though everything had changed. Dad was very worried about the family in Israel. They were all worried. But Dad had completely changed from fun, friendly Dad into grumpy, miserable, hardly ever at home Dad. Tamara often felt grumpy herself these days. But she mostly avoided Dad and getting into arguments with him. However, last night was the bitter end. How did my whole life go so wrong in a few short minutes? she asked herself over and over. As she stared at her phone, Tamara could hear mum's voice again in her ear, as they sat at the table last night.

"Girls," Mum had said. "We have something to tell you."

Dad looked serious and Mum looked worried.

Now what? wondered Tamara. There was so

much bad news these days, she tried not to listen. All she wanted to do was finish dinner and message Yaz. Eden, her little sister, put her thumb in her mouth which she did now whenever she was worried. It infuriated Mum. "What can you expect?" Tamara had told her mother. "You and Dad are always on your phones, your voices are either angry or upset and Eden doesn't get it. So, she sucks her thumb. It's obvious." Tamara had rolled her eyes which probably wasn't a good idea, but she was fed up with all the phone calls too.

"I'm worried about her top teeth coming through properly," Mum had answered, in a prim voice.

"She's only six," Tamara had said. Who cared about teeth when her baby sister was sad!

Since October 7th and the horrific attack on Israel, all Mum and Dad seemed to do was scroll on their phones, make video calls to the family in Israel and watch the news.

They'd all been frightened of course, and here in London there were nasty things against Jews too, which Tamara found quite scary. But more recently, she'd felt as though the family had gone off into separate corners and she wasn't allowed to ask any questions or watch the news. She looked things up online of course but it was all very confusing and there was no one to talk to at home.

We don't know how to *be* together anymore, she told herself.

Dad didn't look up from his phone at mealtimes, except to say something harsh to Tamara like don't eat with your mouth open and Mum didn't even tell him to put his phone away. Which is totally against the rules, Tamara would rage to herself. *I'm* not allowed to bring my phone to the table.

Now Mum fixed her eyes on Dad as if for support and said, "Your cousin Gidi is being sent over from Israel to stay with us."

"What!" said Tamara. "Why? For how long!"

Are they serious? shot through her mind. Where would he sleep? He's such a silly little kid.

"We don't know for how long," Mum went on. "A few weeks, maybe. His dad, your uncle David, has been called up because of the war. He's a reserve medic in the army. Aunty Sharon is in hospital. There's no one to look after Gidi." Then she said very quickly, "He'll have your room of course, Tamara, it's only fair, and you'll share with Eden."

"Oh," said Eden, round her thumb, her face rather blotchy, which always happened when she was tired.

But Tamara's chilli temper exploded like volcanic lava. "No way! This is NEVER gonna happen! A boy . . ." Her voice almost cracked with the effort. "A boy in my room, going through my stuff, are you insane. I absolutely refuse and won't ever . . ."

"Quiet, Tamara!" Dad had snapped.

The room fell silent, except for the sound of Eden sucking furiously.

What Dad said next sliced through Tamara like a piece of glass.

"What a shocking way to behave towards your own family! I'm so disappointed."

Tears sprang to Tamara's eyes as she stared down at her plate.

"Your uncle David – my little brother . . ." Dad's voice broke with emotion, but he forced himself to continue, "and Aunty Sharon have been through a nightmare with Gidi and Keren, trying to keep them safe. You've stayed every summer in their lovely apartment in Haifa. Keren always shares her room with you."

Tamara could only nod. Keren was fifteen and had introduced Tamara to awesome bands and a really cool influencer on social media. Keren was always messaging make-up tips. Tamara hung on her older cousin's every word.

"Imagine air raid sirens going off twenty times a day," Dad went on. "They have to run down six floors to the bomb shelter; they're not allowed to use the lift in an air raid."

Dad's grey eyes, edged with fear, were boring into Tamara and she felt quite frightened as he went on and on.

"Imagine being so terrified you're going to be hit by a bomb. And it wasn't just on October 7th. The sirens have been going off ever since. No one knows when or where rockets will fall. They're hitting towns all over the country. Our family and everyone in Israel are living through this and what about the children?"

Tamara froze. What does he want me to say? she thought as tears trickled down her face.

But Dad didn't soften. He charged on, "The children were stuck at home, couldn't go to school, couldn't see their friends . . ."

"You'd hate that, Tamara," Mum had cut in. "Not seeing your friends."

Tamara was grateful for Mum's kinder voice and gave a small nod.

It wasn't the right time to point out all the Covid lockdowns when she thought she'd go mad, stuck indoors with Eden and her parents.

Dad carried on slicing and slicing into Tamara with his words, telling her how ungrateful she was, and didn't she know how lucky she was to be safe here in London.

I'm so mean, she told herself, as she let out a quiet sob. Oh, why couldn't she take back her words? Go back in time a few minutes and think before she spoke. But it was too late.

Finally, Dad ran out of steam and snapped, "Go to your room."

Tears pouring down her cheeks, Tamara ran off upstairs, into her bedroom and threw herself on the bed. She cried for what seemed hours. Then the door opened a crack and Eden's small, round face, thumb in her mouth, appeared. Her cheeks were stained with tears too. Tamara opened her arms and Eden ran in, jumped on the bed and cuddled up close.

"I don't know why everyone's so angry," said Eden in a sad voice. "You can sleep in my room, Tamsy. Only not in my bed."

That made Tamara smile through her tears and smoothing down Eden's fine light hair, she said, "Don't worry, EdieBoo. We'll drag in the chair bed Yaz sleeps on when we have sleepovers."

Eden gave a satisfied sigh and closed her eyes.

I'm so mean, Tamara thought as she watched Eden sleep. Dad said so and Mum didn't stick up for me, so she probably thinks the same. And what about Yaz, Josh and Arthur?

Whatever happened she mustn't let her friends know what she said last night.

Her thoughts were broken now by the bell.

"Does your cousin play football?" Arthur asked, swinging his school pack onto his shoulder.

"We'll help you look after him," said Josh.

The boys walked off. Tamara's heart was beating as she waited for Yaz to push her phone down into the bottom of her bag and straighten up.

"Oh, Tam," said Yaz, in a voice so full of sympathy, Tamara felt tears start again. "Your room."

Yaz understands, Tamara told herself, even more relieved she hadn't been honest about the row last night and the two friends linked arms to go to class.

* * *

It was a busy day in school, including Library duties, and Tamara didn't have time to catch up with her friends.

"Walk home together?" she said to Yaz as they met at the lockers after school.

"Extra band practice," said Yaz. "See you tomorrow."

Tamara almost felt relieved as she walked towards the school gates. No-one has guessed and by tomorrow, she told herself, things'll be OK. I'll try to be nice to Gidi even if I hate him taking over my room. The truth was, her anger had hovered just below the surface all day. She'd searched around for keys to lock drawers the night before, but she couldn't find any. That cousin of mine better not go through my stuff, she told herself. I know he's been through a rotten time – and a pang went through her again at how she could never take back her mean words – but it doesn't give him an excuse to invade my privacy.

She walked out of school, her coat hanging open as school had been so stuffy all day, making her feel even more miserable. Then she saw Becky, one of the Jewish girls in her year, up ahead.

Becky was small for her age with a mass of dark hair and at nearly twelve had never been on a sleepover. Some of the girls called her 'the baby'. But Tamara and Yaz liked Becky.

"Hey," Tamara called out, joining the smaller girl.

"Walk to the bus stop with me?" said Becky.

"Sure," said Tamara and they set off down the road together, chattering away.

As they turned down one of the quieter streets away from school, two men appeared and came to a halt, blocking their way. Tamara stopped, surprised, and instinctively reached for Becky's arm.

"Oi, you!" said one of the men. "Get off the pavement."

At first, Tamara felt puzzled as she stared at the men. They had pale, round faces and were dressed in jeans and denim jackets with black baseball caps pulled low over their foreheads. Becky tugged Tamara's arm to pull her away. But Tamara's temper flared, and she called out in a defiant voice, "We can walk here if we want."

"We said move," the other man snarled. "This ain't a Jew pavement."

He pointed a thick finger at Tamara's neck.

Shocked, she reached up and to her horror, felt her gold Star outside her sweater on full show. Oh no! she thought. It must have slipped out and I haven't zipped up my coat today.

Mum had told her never to wear the Star in the street. "It's not safe since October 7th. Jewish men have been attacked just for wearing a kippa."

Then Becky wrenched Tamara's arm almost out of its socket and the two girls ran across the road and round the corner to Becky's bus stop.

"OMG, Bex!" burst out Tamara. "Those racist pigs!"

Becky was trembling with fear and her face had gone very white.

"Why did you have your Star on show?" said Becky, in a voice close to tears.

"I'm so sorry," said Tamara. "I didn't mean it. It must have slipped out. We should report them."

"No," said Becky. "Mum and Dad have only just let me come to school on my own. I'm not saying anything."

The bus drew up a few moments later and Becky was gone.

Tamara walked home, even more angry than she'd been on the walk to school that morning. But she felt the same as Becky. I'm in so much trouble already, she thought. Mum and Dad will only say it was all my fault with those men.

Becky's last words, just before she hopped on the bus, rang in her ears.

"My mum says this country will never be the same again after October 7th."

"For us Jews," Tamara had hissed after her, as the bus rolled off.

2

Ten Pencils in a Row

By Thursday morning Gidi was installed in Tamara's room.

Tamara was sleeping on the chair bed in Eden's tiny bedroom, her face crammed up against the wall. Eden was over excited about all the changes and kept trying to give Gidi things, like a necklace she'd strung out of coloured beads.

Gidi had hardly said a word.

He'd arrived very late on Wednesday evening. Dad had collected him from the airport, but the plane was three hours late.

As her cousin came into the house, Tamara's heart sank.

Gidi was as small as she remembered, not yet five foot. His hair fell in ragged clumps over his face and almost down to his shoulders. Tamara thought it looked weird and was sure he'd worn it much shorter last time she saw him.

Gidi had golden brown skin like her father and Uncle David. His arms and legs were very thin and there were purple bruises under his eyes. Tamara couldn't help noticing how scruffy her cousin looked in a grubby T-shirt, jean shorts equally grubby, and scuffed trainers with no socks. He's a proper mess, thought Tamara, her heart sinking even further. What will the kids say in school?

"Come in, darling," Mum had said in her soft voice, and she'd wrapped the boy in a gentle hug. But Gidi stood there like a robot, arms hanging by his side, not speaking.

"We're very glad you're here, Gidi. Aren't we, girls?" Mum had said in a bright voice, drawing back and giving Gidi a concerned look.

She glared at Tamara.

Prompted, Tamara had replied, "Yes, course. Um . . . no worries, Gidi. I'll look after you."

Gidi kept his eyes lowered to the floor.

"Me too, Gidsy!" Eden had cried out, jumping up and down as if her feet had springs.

Gidi had raised his eyes then and stared at the little girl. But he stayed silent.

What am I going to do with him? Tamara thought. How's he gonna cope in school and Mum says I have to take him tomorrow.

"Can't he just stay at home for a bit?" she'd said to Mum the night before.

"Don't be ridiculous, Tamara," Mum had snapped back and that was the end of it.

After the hug, Mum had led Gidi upstairs and into Tamara's room.

That was so awful. Mum and Eden and Gidi all crammed into her bedroom, looking at all her stuff. Tamara felt as if she'd been invaded by aliens. She'd already tried to move some of her things into Eden's room but there was so little space. Some of her schoolbooks were in a box at the end of the narrow chair bed and her laptop was in another box on top of the books. She'd have to do her homework sitting on the bed and Eden was so excited to be sharing, she'd probably be in the room the whole time.

I've nowhere to go, thought Tamara. And no one cares. Mum dropped Gidi's small suitcase onto Tamara's bed and said, "Let's unpack your things." But when she opened the case, it was almost empty. "Gidi, darling, where's your underwear?"

Mum rooted through, holding up a couple of t-shirts, a pair of socks, a faded pair of jeans and a baseball hat which Gidi took from her and crammed on his head.

Tamara spotted two books in Hebrew at the bottom of the case. They had interesting covers, but she couldn't read Hebrew. She was useless at languages and had picked up very few Hebrew words when they were in Israel. Suddenly she couldn't even remember if Gidi spoke English and a sense of panic swept through her when she pictured taking him to school the next day.

Then Mum said, "Who packed for you, darling? Dad? Keren?"

In a tiny voice Gidi said, "I packed. Dad was busy with army stuff. Keren had already gone to Nava's."

"Oh yes," said Mum in an enthusiastic tone. "It was lovely of Nava's family to let her stay with them. They'll look after your sister, don't worry. The girls have important exams this year." Mum frowned again at the little heap of clothes. Almost to herself, she said, "I'll take you shopping on Saturday." She nodded over to Tamara.

But Tamara was too busy with her thoughts to nod back. She'd had such a rush of relief as she heard Gidi's voice. It was the one she recognised from their last trip to Haifa, more than a year ago.

Gidi and Keren spoke fluent English because their parents, Uncle David and Aunty Sharon, were English. Uncle David was Dad's younger brother, by almost four years. David and Sharon had gone to live in Israel when they got married. Uncle David was offered a super new job at the main hospital in Haifa.

"Anyway, we've both wanted to make Aliyah, you know, go and live in Israel, since our teens," explained Aunty Sharon.

Sharon and David had met in a Jewish club and Mum was always telling Tamara she should go to the synagogue club, to meet other Jewish children.

"But Yaz can't come," Tamara would say. "We go to Spotlight Club with all our friends. Some of them are Jewish."

"You could go to both," Mum had said.

Tamara's cousins, Keren and Gidi, had been born in Israel, but their parents made sure their English was perfect. Now Tamara noticed that Gidi's voice had broken which was quite early. Josh's was still high pitched and even Arthur's hadn't properly broken yet.

That'll help in school, she told herself.

The next morning, at breakfast, Gidi was wearing a different, less grubby T-shirt, the baseball cap and jeans. Mum had promised to get his uniform on Saturday.

But he'll look odd at school until then, Tamara thought.

Tamara felt as washed out as Gidi's clothes. She'd hardly had any sleep on the narrow chair bed. Confused thoughts rolled round her head as she lay awake, tossing and turning. Why hadn't Dad tried to make up? What was going to happen when she took Gidi to school? She missed her bedroom so much she ached inside.

Tamara usually had a big bowl of cereal and toast for breakfast but this morning it was as though her throat had closed.

Mum was too busy to notice. "Tamara, listen, please."

Tamara gave an inward sigh and looked up.

"You have to lock up the house today," Mum went

on. "Dad's already gone to work and I have to take Eden to school earlier because I have an appointment. You're in charge of Gidi."

Tamara had hardly seen Dad since the awful row on Tuesday evening, almost two days ago. He's avoiding me, she thought, feeling quite sad.

Mum broke into her thoughts. "Tamara? Did you hear me?"

"Yes," said Tamara in a weary voice. "You finished, Gidi?"

Her cousin gave a small nod. He hadn't eaten anything either. She made a mental note to make sure he ate lunch. Mum would be furious if Gidi had nothing all day.

Mum and Eden went off and Tamara heard the car start.

Pushing back her chair, she scraped her plate into the bin and put it in the dishwasher. Then she picked up Gidi's plate and mug, still full, and did the same.

"OK," she said, wiping her hands on a tea towel. "Let's go," and she went into the hall.

Gidi followed her. There were hooks near the front door, crammed with the family's coats. Tamara rummaged through and found a winter jacket she'd grown out of. She held it out to her cousin. "It's cold out there," she muttered.

Gidi took the jacket, put it on and zipped it up to his chin. He still looked miserable. But at least it was khaki green and didn't look too girly. Another item for the Gidi clothes list, Tamara told herself as she put on her own jacket. Wonder if I'll get anything.

But she didn't hold out any hope. She was in everyone's bad books right now.

"You'll do," she said to Gidi. "Come on."

They walked to school in silence. It was a cold, crisp November morning, with a clear blue sky streaked with thin white clouds. Tamara's favourite winter weather. It made her want to run, her long legs loping up to the main road and all the way to school.

But this morning she had to walk with Gidi and he was only shuffling along, head down, baseball cap hiding his face, hands shoved deep in pockets.

Tamara sighed and walked on, slightly ahead until they reached the school gates.

"We've just got time to go to my locker and then it's Maths," she said.

But at the lockers, Gidi refused to take off his baseball cap. He let Tamara put away his coat.

Tamara collected her books for the first lesson. Double Maths with Miss Tate. A tall, square woman in her thirties, Miss Tate taught in a rushed, irritated voice, expecting the class to keep up. She never went over a point a second time. Miss Tate had favourites too and Tamara and Josh were definitely not in that category.

Josh shrugged it off. "Who cares? Plenty of teachers are OK."

But Tamara felt her temper rising in every Maths class.

"I don't know what I've done wrong," she'd said to Mum and Dad at dinner in the second week of term. "She told me today I never listen. It's just not true. So unfair."

"You're in high school, now," Dad had said. "You're going to meet lots of new people, more adults and kids than you've ever met before. Some of them won't be fair. Keep your head down and get through."

Tamara thought he was right, but she was still angry that Miss Tate picked on her.

Now as she led Gidi into class and they both sat down at a table, Yaz called out from the back row. Swivelling round, Tamara started to chat with her friend, leaving Gidi to sort himself out until the teacher arrived. Suddenly a familiar voice bellowed across the room, "You kidding me! Hey Dean, you seen this muppet?"

It was the dreaded Lola with Dean, the meanest pair in Year 7 and Lola was pushing her way towards Tamara.

But it wasn't Tamara she was pointing her finger at. It was Gidi.

To Tamara's horror she saw that her cousin had brought a pencil case with him – like, where had he hidden that? she couldn't help thinking.

He'd emptied the contents onto the tabletop. But not in a muddled heap, like anyone else would have done. Gidi had lined up with precision spacing, three red pencils, three yellow pencils, three blue pencils and one lead pencil with an unused eraser on the end. Each pencil was sharpened to a perfect point and Gidi was sitting with his arms folded, very upright, staring at the table.

"What a weirdo!" Dean yelled back and the whole class turned to look.

Then to Tamara's even greater horror, Dean swept all the pencils onto the floor in one move.

A spike of anger went up through her.

She pushed her chair back and shouted, "Leave my cousin alone, you bully."

She heard Yaz call her name out, but the red-hot chilli temper was racing to the surface.

"Your cousin," scoffed Dean. "Another weirdo then. And what's that on your cap, muppet?"

Gidi hadn't moved but that frozen look was on his face, the one Tamara had seen last night and his body had reverted to robot mode.

What's wrong with him? Tamara thought.

Lola's next words made Tamara freeze too.

"It's Hebrew, innit," Lola almost spat out.

Dean curled up his mouth, pointed at Gidi and said in a mocking voice, "You're Israel."

Lola started chanting, "Is-rael. Is-rael. Is-rael."

Dean joined in and so did a group of mean girls who followed Lola around.

That was too much for Tamara. Her temper reached boiling point and she launched herself at Dean. At that moment Miss Tate entered the class and shouted, "Head's office, Tamara Cohen. Sit down, Dean and Lola, and who on earth is that!"

She waved a ruler towards Gidi, who didn't flicker an eyelash.

"Remove that hat or leave my classroom!" barked the teacher.

Still in a fury, Tamara grabbed her cousin and dragged him out of the room.

3

Lunch Break

"I had a long conversation with your mother this morning, Tamara."

Mrs Cole, the Head, was sitting at her desk, gazing at Tamara and Gidi, who stood on the opposite side. "And now Miss Tate says you've been fighting in class."

Tamara frowned, feeling confused and defiant all at the same time.

"I know all about your cousin coming to stay. From Haifa, I believe, in the north of Israel." Mrs Cole gave Gidi a kind look. "This must be all very strange for you, Gideon. But it's good you are staying with your family and your aunty Mel assures me you will have all your uniform this weekend. That will help you to fit in."

Gidi stayed in robot mode.

Tamara said, "Yes, Miss. Thank you, Miss. Sorry, Miss."

Mrs Cole transferred the gaze to Tamara, who was

clutching the sides of her skirt to try to stop trembling. This was the first time in her life she'd been sent to the Head.

Will I be suspended? she wondered, a feeling of dread in the pit of her stomach.

Mrs Cole was speaking again. "Tamara, that temper of yours. I know Dean and Lola are not the best-behaved pupils, but I cannot condone fighting."

There was a pause and in the silence Tamara thought, I'm in trouble everywhere.

But she decided to try to speak up.

"Lola and Dean were mocking Gidi," she said in a small voice, "because of his cap. They called him Israel as if . . . as if it's a rude word and that's not fair, Miss."

Mrs Cole gave an understanding nod. "These are difficult times for you and your community, I know. I will be speaking to Lola and Dean too." The Head moved some papers on her desk and then she said, "Gideon, you can't wear a baseball cap in school. Take it off please and put it on my desk. I'll make sure you have it to take home."

Gidi's face crumpled and he looked close to tears.

For the first time, Tamara felt a touch of sympathy for her cousin.

He must have been so scared back in class, she thought.

She gave him a nudge. "Come on, Gidi," she murmured.

Slowly Gidi removed the cap and put it on the Head's desk. "It belongs to Abba," he said in a quiet voice.

"Abba means Dad," explained Tamara, relieved she knew that word in Hebrew. "His dad's a medic in the army, in the Negev Brigade, like it says on the cap."

Gidi nodded.

Mrs Cole stared at Gidi for a moment and then she said, "Tamara, I think it would be best if you and Gideon sit out lessons this morning in the library. Take your books and go through some Maths. I know that your English is excellent, Gideon, which will be very helpful fitting in at school." She gave the boy an encouraging smile.

Relief flooded through Tamara. No suspension, she thought.

Before Tamara could thank the Head, there was a knock at the door and without waiting the door opened.

Arthur's face appeared. "Please, Miss. Sorry, Miss. I brought Gidi's pencil case."

Gidi's face lit up and he bounded across the room.

How ridiculous, thought Tamara. It's only an old pencil case.

But Gidi grabbed the case and zipped it open, checking the contents.

"It's all there, mate," said Arthur. "Might need to sharpen a couple. The points broke."

Then Arthur disappeared and Mrs Cole said, "Well I'm not sure what that was all about, but good to see a smile on your face, young man."

Gidi ducked his head.

"We do things differently here, Gideon. But Tamara and her friends will be helpful, I'm sure. Now off you both go. And Tamara."

"Yes, Miss?"

"You're on a warning. Keep that temper of yours under control."

"Yes, Miss. I will, Miss. Thank you, Miss."

Once they were settled at a table in the library, Tamara said, "What's it all about with those pencils, Gids?"

"My sister gave them to me," said Gidi, as he emptied the case again and lined up all the pencils in exactly the same way as before.

"But why do you do . . ." Tamara waved a hand towards the pencils. ". . . do that?"

Gidi shrugged, folded his arms and stared at the table.

Tamara gave an inward sigh. He's almost a year younger than me and the others, she reminded herself. But the pencils irritated her.

To take her mind off things, Tamara opened her Maths book and went through some of the pages, setting Gidi a few problems.

Gidi did surprisingly well.

He's quite clever, really, she thought.

The morning passed quickly in the peace and quiet of

the library and then the bell for lunch went. Tamara gathered up her books. Hearing her name, she looked up to see Josh and Arthur striding through the library.

"Thought we'd take Gidi to lunch," said Arthur, putting his arm loosely round the smaller boy's shoulders and guiding him towards the door. Gidi had already tidied away all his things, including the annoying pencils, and he seemed happy to go with Arthur and Josh. Relieved of Gidi duty as she called it in her mind, Tamara went off into the lunchroom, finding Yaz at a table near the wall.

"What did the Head say?" said Yaz.

"It was OK," said Tamara. "Sent us to the library to study. I hate Miss Tate; she's always picking on me. She never picks on you."

"Or Dean and Lola," said Yaz with a nod. "Gidi all right?"

Tamara gave a weary nod towards the queue, where Gidi was standing with Josh and Arthur. "I'm having a break from baby watching."

"Bit harsh, Tam," said Yaz and they both burst into giggles.

But Tamara could hardly believe her eyes when the boys came back and Gidi put his tray down. He had two huge burgers in buns and another plate piled high with chips.

"Seriously!" she said to Josh and Arthur who were both grinning.

"We told them he's a new boy, just arrived in the

country and hasn't eaten for three days," said Arthur.

"You should have heard the dinner ladies," said Josh, "*Oh, poor little lovey,*" he mimicked. "*Must be proper starving.*"

"Yeah, I thought they were gonna take him home," said Arthur, squeezing ketchup onto his plate.

"You'll never eat all that, Gidi," said Tamara.

But to her amazement Gidi ploughed his way through the entire meal.

"Unbelievable!" said Tamara. "I'm gonna message Mum, tell her to get in extra supplies. She'll love feeding you up, cousin."

Gidi shrugged. Then he pushed his plate aside, lifted up his T-shirt and wiped his mouth.

"Er, not sure that's a good idea," said Josh, checking no one else noticed.

"My abba does it," said Gidi. "And his friends."

"Well, we don't do that in London," snapped Tamara.

Gidi's face fell and to Tamara's annoyance, he took out his pencil case, lined up all his pencils in precision order and folded his arms, a vacant look on his face.

"What're we gonna do about this?" whispered Tamara to Yaz.

"The neighbour says her sister washes her hands over thirty times a day," Yaz whispered back. "She gets stressed."

"Is he stressed, then?" said Tamara. "I suppose it's all my fault as usual."

Yaz gave her a puzzled look and Tamara remembered she hadn't told the others about how mean she'd been and the row with Dad.

But maybe Gidi is all wound up because of me, she thought. His sister gave him those pencils and I can't imagine Keren doing anything dumb like lining them up. So maybe he only started when he saw me and somehow he knows I didn't want him to come and stay.

Her heart sank.

But then she felt Yaz's cool hand on her arm and heard her say, "Course it isn't. I bet he's been doing it for weeks. Life's a bit stressful in Israel at the moment, isn't it?"

Tamara gave a sigh. "Yeah. Whatever. Let's get him outside. He can kick a ball about with Arthur and I'll hold his flipping pencil case."

It was a dry afternoon and Tamara, Gidi and the others headed through the doors and outside to the Year 7 area. This was a large space with a basketball stand, five-a-side nets and benches and tables, where the girls usually sat.

"I'll look after your bag," said Tamara in a firm voice to Gidi, sliding the strap off the boy's shoulder. "You go with Josh and Arthur."

Gidi hesitated and Josh said, "Come on, mate. They're only gonna talk boring girl stuff."

Arthur dropped his football in Gidi's arms and Gidi clutched it.

"Throw it and we'll start a game," Arthur said, smiling at the smaller boy.

To Tamara's surprise, Gidi threw the ball halfway down the area, towards the football net. Half a dozen boys and a couple of girls appeared. They fell into two teams without a word, Gidi playing with Josh and Arthur and a rough sort of game started.

"Phew," said Tamara as she sat down with Yaz, Becky and Becky's friend, Hannah, another Jewish girl. "Five minutes' peace."

"So," said Hannah. "Becky's party, Saturday."

The girls all huddled round.

"Dad says we have to end at nine," said Becky.

"Bor-ing," said Hannah.

"I'm working on my mum," said Becky with a grin. "It involves lots of looking after my little brother but I think I've almost cracked it. She's so desperate for some peace and quiet, she's almost agreed to going on until eleven."

"Awesome," said Tamara. "Can I bring my cousin?" She nodded over to the football game.

"Course," said Becky in a generous voice. "He seems nice."

Tamara stared at her friend, but then she realised that Becky was quite a small person too, probably even shorter than Gidi and although she was about to turn twelve, she still liked to play with dolls as well as trying on make-up.

She likes him, Tamara thought with an inward shrug.

She turned away to watch the boys and heard Josh call out Gidi's name.

Looking round she saw Gidi suddenly accelerate past three bigger boys, put his foot out and kick the ball towards Arthur. Arthur caught the ball on the run with his foot, raced down the pitch and slammed it into the back of the net.

"Gi-di! Gi-di!" went up a chant around the boys and several of them patted Gidi on the back.

Tamara felt her shoulders relax. It's gonna be OK, she told herself and turned back as the other girls chatted about outfits for Becky's party.

4

Warrior Gran

It was Friday night and Gran was coming over.

It was two years since Grandad Jonny had died and Tamara still missed him. They were Mum's parents. She'd never known her other set of grandparents. So, Gran was even more precious now, as the last one left.

Tamara's job on Friday nights was to put out the silver candlesticks with white candles, lay the plaited challah loaf on the bread board which was only used on Shabbat and bring the large silver knife from the sideboard drawer.

"Careful! Don't cut your finger!" Mum said every week.

Only this Shabbat, Mum was barely speaking to her.

It's only been three days since the row but I'm permanently in the doghouse, Tamara moaned to herself. So unfair.

Once the challah and knife were on the board, Tamara covered them with a special cloth. *Shabbat Shalom* was embroidered on the cloth in blue and white thread, the colours of the Israeli flag. When she was four, Tamara had asked Grandad Jonny, "Why do we cover the challah?"

"So, we don't embarrass it," Grandad had answered, with a twinkle in his eye.

Tamara had giggled and said, "You can't embarrass bread."

"Yes, you can," said Grandad. "We drink the wine first and we make the challah wait. So, we have to cover it or it might go all red in the face."

Everyone had laughed.

But when she was older, Tamara read about it in a book and saw that Grandad was right, along with several other reasons for the challah cover.

Her last Friday night job was to put out the silver kiddush cup. Mum would fill the cup with kosher wine later. Then Tamara laid out cutlery, plates, glasses and napkins and her job was done for another week. She usually stood for a moment, proud to see how she had created such a nice table for the family but this Shabbat evening she just slumped down on the sofa, pushed in her earbuds and listened to music on her mobile. There was nowhere to go until dinner because Gidi was in her room, and she didn't want to sit on her bed with Eden.

"Have you taken all your, like, personal stuff?" Yaz

had said that morning in school.

"Not much room for me in Eden's room," grumbled Tamara. "My diary's under my pillow."

Yaz had nodded with sympathy. "You can sleepover at mine whenever you want."

But Yaz had three sisters and shared a room with Ayisha who was nine. Tamara would have to roll up in a sleeping bag on the cramped floor space between the two beds.

Worse than sharing with Eden, she told herself.

"Thanks. Maybe," she said.

Yaz gave an understanding nod.

Tamara's thoughts were interrupted by the jangle of the doorbell and rushing down the hall, she opened the door and threw herself into Gran's arms.

Grandma Helen was short like mum, just over five foot, with a broad comfortable frame which cushioned Tamara's body as it always had. She was almost seventy-five and Eden said aloud more than once, "That's ancient, Gran, like the dinosaurs," which made Gran laugh. Grandma Helen had the same frizzy hair as Mum and Tamara. Eden's hair was quite fine and straight, a dusty brown like dad. Gran kept her hair short and coloured reddish with henna to cover up her grey hairs. Her small dark eyes moved around quick as a bird's and missed nothing. Now she gave Tamara a hug and whispered in her ear, "I love you, darling."

Gran is on my side, Tamara thought. She tugged

her grandmother down to the dining room, not wanting to let go and sat beside her.

Dad took his place at the top of the table, Eden and Gidi either side.

Then Mum stood up. She held up a small packet in her hand. "They were giving them out at the synagogue when I popped in this morning to drop off a bag for the foodbank."

"What is it?" said Gran.

"Candles. They're asking everyone to light them to remember the hostages hidden away in Gaza," said Mum.

"What's a hostage?" asked Eden.

Tamara caught Gidi's eye and he dipped his head, his ragged hair almost touching the plate.

The hostages had been kidnapped on October 7th by Hamas, from Israel during the attacks and had been hidden away in Gaza for weeks. Everyone was worried about them.

Even me, Tamara told herself. Then she had a terrible thought. Does Gidi know someone kidnapped and stuffed down in a tunnel? But I daren't ask. Dad will shout at me.

Her shoulders slumped and she stared at her plate.

Then Dad said, "A hostage is someone who's been taken from their home and we don't know where they are." Before Eden could say anything else, Dad went on, "Good idea, Mel. Light them too."

Mum lit the two small blue candles which she

placed on a dish and then the two white candles in the candlesticks. She covered her eyes and stood there for a moment, as if giving a special space to the hostages. Then she said the prayer and sat down.

Tamara felt very serious and solemn and glad that they were finally actually *doing* something. She'd felt powerless since the October 7th attack on Israel, although it did feel very far away from London. But everything had changed this week. First those men who blocked her way on the street with Becky and then the horrible racism in school. Tamara felt as though the war was right inside her own life now and not just a war far away in Israel.

Those words, "Move. This ain't a Jew pavement," rang through her head over and over again. She found herself checking her Star of David was out of sight under her sweater all the time now.

I want to fight back, she told herself as she stared at the candles for the hostages. But what can a twelve-year-old girl do?

Dad recited the prayers over the wine and challah. Then he stood up and said, as he always did every Friday night, "Come here, children."

Tamara pushed back her chair as Eden took Gidi's hand and pulled him over to stand next to Dad. But in a sort of helpless gesture, Dad shrugged, raising his hands, palms up. "I only have two," he said. He placed one hand on Eden's head and one on Gidi's, as he recited the blessing. Tamara couldn't help feeling a bit pushed out. But I'm the eldest, she told herself, and it's right Gidi has my usual place.

All her life she'd stood on Friday nights with Dad's warm palm on her head, with him saying the exact same blessing, the one to keep children safe.

Tonight Gidi needed her place. But she couldn't help feeling a bit sad.

As Dad recited the familiar prayer, "May God bless you and keep you . . ." tears welled in Tamara's eyes. Then she felt Gran's broad hand on her head. Gran had come over to be with Tamara and she felt herself relax a little. What else could Dad do, now that Gidi is here? Tamara told herself. But, to be honest, nothing felt the same.

Once Mum had dished up dinner, Gran launched into a story.

"So last Saturday night we all went out – me, Harvey and Linda from the Lunch Bunch in our shul and Maurice Cohen, who's always up for anything. You know Maurice," said Gran to Mum who nodded back with a grin.

"Where did you lot go?" said Dad, raising an eyebrow towards Mum.

"Trafalgar Square," said Gran.

Dad spluttered and nearly spat out half a roast potato.

Eden gave a loud giggle and even Gidi grinned.

Tamara kept her eyes on her plate, her lips twitching.

"What the heck are you doing there on a Saturday evening! In the middle of London for heaven's sake!" cried out Dad.

"Mum!" said Mum at almost the same time. "Are you crazy? All those demonstrators yelling Free Palestine and Global Intifada. Some of them get really nasty. You know they pushed over a Jewish boy last week because he held up a poster about Hamas. The police told the Jewish boy he was being provocative."

"We don't care," said Gran, raising her round chin in defiance. "Me, Harvey and the others are really fed up. This is our city. Why can't we walk about in our own city, in our own country, anytime we want? Jews are British citizens too, right, kids?"

"Right, gransy pansy," said Eden with a giggle.

Tamara knew Eden didn't understand a word.

She was about to open her mouth and agree with Gran when she caught Mum's eye. Mum gave a little shake of her head. Tamara frowned but she didn't say anything.

Dad was about to speak but Gran cut him off.

"Now, listen, Ben." She held up her hand, arm outstretched, palm facing towards Dad.

Tamara thought, that's telling him. Gran's a superhero.

"We didn't walk in the middle of them," Gran continued. "We especially steered clear of those people who cover up their faces and put sunglasses over their eyes."

Gran was getting into her stride. Tamara felt quite excited, as though something was finally happening. Maybe I can go with them sometime, she thought.

"We took up a position near the steps to the National Gallery," went on Gran. "Then Maurice and Harvey held up a large Israeli flag."

"Mum!" said Mum again, in the same high pitched, horrified voice. "That'll make them angry."

Gran ignored her. "After a few minutes, a group of kids came over with those black and white check keffiyeh scarves over their mouths. They had to shout, otherwise you couldn't hear what they were saying." Gran's small eyes glittered with fun. "Linda was filming it all on her mobile. She posted it on her social media," said Gran, nodding at Tamara.

"Cool," said Tamara.

Mum gasped and shook her head.

Dad tutted.

Gran ignored them and went on, "Those kids were yelling all the slogans – Free Palestine, From the River to the Sea – and they don't even know which river or which sea," said Gran. "Maurice asked a couple of girls waving a Palestinian flag. They wore sweaters from their universities, so they're supposed to be clever," said Gran in a sarcastic voice. "But they looked at each other all bewildered and then one said, 'Um, is it the Nile, and the Atlantic?'"

Dad almost choked on his potato again, but Tamara cried out, "That's what Josh said in school this week.

He says they all watch stuff about Gaza on the socials but none of them know it's the River Jordan and the Mediterranean Sea."

"That's my granddaughter," said Gran with pride.

Tamara glowed but she was careful not to meet Dad's eye.

"Always know your facts," went on Gran. "Don't repeat anything you're not sure of."

"Right, Gran," said Tamara.

Now I've got a proper job to do, she thought. Watch the news every night and check all my facts. That'll show Dean and Lola. Bet they don't know which river and which sea.

"Some of them said nasty things about us, as you can imagine," Gran went on. "But what we did . . . you won't believe it. *We* smiled at them the whole time and said, 'Thank you, yes, thank you for coming and speaking to us. Oh yes, very interesting. What else do you want to say?'"

"Way to go, Gran!" Tamara cried out. "Bet that shocked them. They probably thought you'd shout insults back."

"They did. How wrong they were."

"Awesome," said Tamara.

"Quiet, Tamara," snapped Dad.

But Gran continued, "They were really confused because we didn't stop, we kept on speaking to them in quiet, polite voices. Maurice was amazing. He was like a gentle bulldozer. In the end the kids ran out of steam and just stood there, looking round at each other for support."

Gran's voice broke down as she started to laugh and then Eden joined in, and Tamara grinned over at Gidi who actually grinned back. Gran got her voice under control again and went on, "In the end they gave up and went back to the march. I'm your Warrior Gran now, kids." Gran pointed a fork round at Tamara, Eden and Gidi. They all nodded back.

"I'm going to stand up to all those bullies and show them that British Jewish citizens have the same rights as everyone else in London." A broad grin spread over Gran's face. "Maurice says we should go to New York if this carries on into the New Year. Huge marches over there."

"No way!" Mum shrieked out. "I'll confiscate your passport!"

But Tamara and Eden had thrown themselves to their feet and were jumping up and down, yelling, "Warrior Gran! Warrior Gran!"

"Come on, Gidsy!" cried out Eden and Gidi joined in.

Mum and Dad exchanged furious looks.

Then Gran pushed her chair back and said in a firm voice, "Right, stop that, Eden and Gideon. Go upstairs until I call you down for dessert."

"Yaay," said Eden. "We can make friendship bracelets." She grabbed Gidi's hand and pulled him out of the room.

"Melanie and Ben," Gran said, nodding to Mum and Dad, "go and sit on the sofa. Tamara and I will clear up." Gran gave Tamara a meaningful stare.

Tamara piled up some plates and carried them into the kitchen. Gran loaded the dishwasher, while Tamara cleared the table. Then Gran closed the kitchen door, walked over to the sink and leaning on it said, "What's wrong, Tamara, darling?"

It all spilled out, the row on Tuesday night, how Dad had gone mad at her.

"I've never seen him like that," Tamara said in a hurt voice. "I was mean about Gidi coming because I've lost my bedroom but honestly, Gran, it's awful sharing with Eden. I haven't got anywhere to do my homework."

Tamara gave her grandmother an appealing look and Gran nodded.

"I am being nice to Gidi, most of the time," Tamara went on in a small voice. "After everything the family in Israel have gone through. Only it's too late now. Dad hates me and Mum ignores me."

Then the floodgates opened and Tamara cried and cried in Gran's arms.

Eventually her sobbing died away.

Gran passed her a teacloth to dry her eyes, and then she said, "Dad doesn't hate you, darling. Trust me. Mum is caught in the middle between the two of you. You're not mean, you're a very kind girl. You said the wrong thing. OK. Everyone makes mistakes. It's not the end of the world."

Tamara didn't speak but a little flicker of hope lit up inside her. Maybe it's not all broken, she thought.

"Everything's changed since October 7th," said Gran. "I think your dad's on edge all the time, worried about your uncle David because David is his little brother. Now David's in the army in the middle of the war. Your dad's probably worried David will get hurt."

"S'pose so," said Tamara.

"I think your dad let out all his anger and fear on you on Tuesday night," said Gran and then she fixed Tamara with a firm look. "That was very unfair."

5

Becky's Party

Saturday morning Mum made bread latkes with the left-over challah. Slices of bread soaked in egg and milk, gently fried, then coated with a mixture of cinnamon and sugar. Gidi's face lit up and he ate three huge slices. "We always have this on Shabbat. Keren and I both want the – um – edge."

"Crust," said Eden. "I love the crust but you can have it today, Gidsy."

Tamara loved the crust too but today she didn't care after another washed-out night on the chair bed. She had no idea where she was going to get ready for Becky's party tonight; Eden's room was too cramped and the bathroom was always busy, especially with an extra person in the house.

I feel like a refugee, she thought.

Gidi seemed to have come alive with breakfast and was saying, "On Shabbat I meet my friend Yussuf.

He's three floors below me. We go over to the park and hang up."

"Hang out," said Tamara in a quiet voice.

Mum offered Gidi another slice.

"*Lo, todah,*" he said.

"*Lo todah,*" mimicked Eden.

"Oh, sorry," said Gidi going red. "I spoke in Ivrit."

"Don't worry, darling," said Mum. "We understand a bit of Hebrew. No thank you, is that right?"

"*Ken,*" said Gidi.

Before he could correct himself in English, Eden cried out, "Ken and Barbie!"

Gidi looked puzzled but Mum said, "That's what Jewish kids say in England when they hear *Ken*, the Ivrit for *Yes*. It's a bit like *Yoffee Toffee.*"

A smile spread across Gidi's face. "We say *Yoffee Toffee* in Israel."

Tamara knew that one. *Yoffe* meant good and it rhymed beautifully with *Toffee*.

After breakfast they all went shopping and Tamara watched as Mum swiped her credit card. She bought Gidi all his uniform, a winter jacket with a thick hood "for our English rain," Mum said, with a grin, as well as casual clothes and several sets of underwear and socks. Tamara was pleased to see Gidi with new stuff, but she felt a real pang when Mum didn't even offer her a new top for the party. Worse still, when Eden pulled them over to the hobby shop for a new set of beads, Mum gave her a five-pound note.

What about me? thought Tamara with another pang, as Eden skipped off into the shop.

She felt a thin, cold hand slip into hers and Gidi said in a low voice, "When Abba sends me money, I'll buy you something. For taking your room."

A warm feeling came over Tamara and she said, "It's OK. But thanks."

Gidi took his hand away and checked his watch. "It's nearly lunchtime in Israel. Yusuff's going for falafel."

Curious, Tamara said, "So this friend, Yussuf, that's a Muslim name, isn't it?"

"Sure," said Gidi.

"I thought . . . well, especially after October 7th . . ." Tamara wasn't sure how to go on.

"You think Jews and Muslims hate each other in Israel," said Gidi. "It's not like that. There are problems, Abba says, but Haifa's always been mixed. Yussuf and I go to the same club with Israeli Jews and Israeli Arabs."

"And your parents don't mind?" Tamara was really surprised.

"*Mah pitom.*"

"What?" said Tamara.

"Ima says it means, No way."

"So, none of the parents mind," said Tamara.

"Omer and Farrah say, when we are all in Club together, this is what peace looks like."

But Mum and Eden were back and there was no time for Tamara to ask about Omer, Farrah or Yussuf or what life was really like in Israel these days. Anyhow, she told herself as they drove home, probably better not to ask. Gidi needs to be kept busy so he doesn't have time for sad thoughts or lining up his pencils. It's like Yaz says, he's stressed or sad or something.

Gidi's mum was still in hospital and his dad was with the army in the south.

"Just as dangerous as the front line," Dad had said to Mum that morning.

There was so much about this war Tamara didn't understand.

When they arrived home, Eden helped Gidi take all his new clothes up to his room. Tamara went into Eden's room to gather up her laptop and books. She'd have to do homework on the dining table. But back downstairs Dad called Gidi to the table. "Your dad's on a video call."

Gidi's face lit up and he raced over.

Eden disappeared and Tamara hovered in the hallway.

"Too early to get ready for the party, darling," came Mum's voice. She was hanging up her coat on the hooks by the front door.

"Have to do my homework," muttered Tamara, waving her laptop. "But there's nowhere to go."

"Don't worry, come with me." Mum led the way upstairs and into the main bedroom, a large light room which ran across the top of the house. She waved over to the corner and said with a smile, "Dad and I sorted this out last night. Just for you."

Tamara stared with astonishment. They'd set up a desk for her, with a pinboard on the wall and an LED lamp, with three different shades of colour, something Tamara had wanted for ages.

"Mum, it's . . ." Tamara choked and felt tears starting. She brushed them away and said in a wobbly voice, "But Dad hates me and I thought you were . . ."

"Never!" said Mum. "Dad's very worried about Uncle David. You need to give him some space at the moment, Tamara. Everything'll be all right. You'll see. Anyway, you need somewhere quiet to work. Eden's a great little sister but she never . . ."

" . . . stops talking!" they finished together and then they burst into laughter.

Mum put her arms around Tamara and Tamara snuggled up close.

"Won't be forever," murmured Mum.

"I know. It's OK," said Tamara, feeling very much the eldest at that moment. She spent the next hour setting up her desk with school stuff and bits from her room which she was missing so much, like her Taylor Swift sunglasses and silly photos of her and Yaz.

The rest of the day passed with lunch, homework and helping Gidi sort out all his stuff for school. Tamara changed for the party in Mum and Dad's room and then Yaz's mum drove them to Becky's house in the evening.

Becky's dad opened the front door and waved them down to a large, brightly lit room at the back. It had a wooden floor and the furniture had been pushed to the sides. Becky and Hannah had planned some fun team games and everyone had to bring a sleeping bag. "But not for a sleepover," Becky had said with a grin.

Yaz had to lend Gidi her older sister's bag.

"Nice jeans," she'd said approvingly when she handed over the rolled-up bag and Gidi had ducked his head. But at least he doesn't look like a refugee anymore, Tamara had told herself, when Gidi appeared in his new clothes. Mum had also taken him for a haircut that morning and Gidi had said in a small voice, "I'd like it the way Josh has it."

Mum looked puzzled and Tamara had said, "He means a two."

The barber nodded and applied the electric razor, slewing off huge swathes of Gidi's thick, ragged hair. Her cousin looked relieved once it had gone. "Abba and me always wear it like this but there was no time for a haircut after . . . you know."

Now Tamara could see they were the first group to arrive, except for Hannah, who was already there. Hannah was also Jewish and she and Becky were best friends. But there was a strange silence in the room and Becky had her arm around Hannah. Yaz and

Tamara exchanged looks and Yaz said, "Everything OK, party girl?"

Becky shook her head. "Hannah just got a text from Mia, her friend from ice skating. They've been going for years."

Tamara nodded. They all knew Mia.

"What did it say?" asked Tamara.

"I can't be your friend anymore," said Hannah in a small voice.

"Why?" asked Gidi.

"Her mum and dad are pro-Palestinian," said Hannah. "They go on the marches. I suppose Mia has to side with her family."

They were silent for a moment and then there were sounds of people arriving at the front door. Josh and Arthur appeared letting off party poppers and shouting Happy Birthday.

They stopped when they saw the sad faces.

"What's up?" said Arthur.

Becky told him and boys both frowned.

"I don't understand," said Gidi. "Are they Muslims?"

"No," said Tamara, with a snort. "But everyone takes sides now. Three girls in our year, not Jewish, stopped talking to me after October 7th. When I see them, they whisper behind their hands and throw mean looks at me. Just because I'm Jewish."

"*Zeh lo tov*," said Gidi and then translated, "That's not good. My best friend in Israel is Yussuf and he's Arab. He has cousins in Gaza. But we're still best friends."

"Like Mustafa in my football team," said Josh. "I play in the Jewish league and Mustafa wanted to join . . ."

"What position?" said Arthur.

"Defence," said Josh. "He brought two of his friends and I know they're all pro-Palestinian but it doesn't matter. We just play football."

"Like me and Yussuf," said Gidi. "We go to the same club." He nodded at Tamara and she nodded back.

"So, we won the cup," went on Josh. "One of the dads always brings champagne when we win, only now he brings fizzy apple for the Muslim dads."

Arthur looked puzzled.

"Muslims don't drink alcohol," explained Yaz.

"I'll miss Mia," said Hannah, in a gloomy voice.

"Come on!" said Becky and she threw herself to her feet and said, "Let's get this party started."

She put on the music system and Taylor Swift belted out her latest song.

Tamara screamed and holding out a small package cried out, "Open my present first!"

Becky took it, ripped off the paper and screamed back when she saw a bracelet with a disc hanging on it which said, *Be More Taylor.*

She pushed it onto her wrist and cried out, "I love it!"

Suddenly the room filled up with all their friends, and Becky's cousins. Becky turned up the music. Josh and Arthur started competing for who could throw up and catch the most popcorn in their mouths.

Becky's parents had a five-bedroom, detached house in a street near the park. It had a huge garden lit up at night and even though it was November and almost frosty outside, the patio doors were flung open. The party spilled in and out of the garden and some of the girls started a race around the trees, yelling to each other. Tamara poured herself a cola and caught sight of Gidi and Becky on the floor, cross legged. They were both stringing beads from a set Becky had been given to make Swiftie bracelets and were deep in conversation.

Becky gets him, Tamara thought. Great.

Now she could focus on her own friends, enjoy the party and not worry about her cousin.

She was about to join the girls racing round the garden when Becky stood up, turned down the music and cried out, "Sleeping bag race! Everyone grab your bags."

There was a lot of shoving and shouting. Josh and Arthur practised sliding across the floor in their socks, sleeping bags wrapped around their shoulders.

"Hey, you two, not like that, come over here," shouted Becky.

Everyone stood against one wall and Becky explained the game.

"In pairs, you get into your bag and on your stomach you race to the opposite wall. Winner gets a prize."

"Me against Gidi!" said Josh, grinning over at Gidi.

"No," said Becky. "Girls against boys."

"OK," said Josh. "Me against Hannah."

Hannah grinned and climbed into her bag.

They lowered themselves onto the floor, Becky blew a whistle and they were off.

Halfway across the room, Josh seemed to get in a tangle even though he was ahead. Hannah won by a metre and everyone cheered. Becky gave her a bottle of bubbles for a prize. The room filled with bubbles and people jumping up to burst them.

"Sorry about Mia," Tamara said to Hannah, as the other girl came over, her hair plastered to her forehead with sweat.

"It's hurtful," said Hannah. "So unnecessary. I'm not fighting anyone."

"I know," said Tamara. "Before we didn't ever talk about politics. Why would we? We're only twelve. Now it's all politics."

Hannah nodded. "All the Jewish kids I know have friends dumping them."

"Depends what their families say, I suppose," said Yaz, in a cautious voice. "My cousin, Kadija, you know . . ." She nodded to Tamara.

Tamara gave a cautious nod back. Kadija was fourteen and in Year 9 at their school. She didn't know that Yaz was close with her older cousin.

"Well Kadija says," went on Yaz, "that the Gaza bombing is too much. Israel should stop."

Tamara threw Yaz a puzzled look but Yaz didn't meet her eye.

What's that all about? Tamara wondered but then it was Gidi's turn to race against Yaz.

Everyone was laughing and jeering as Yaz struggled into her sleeping bag.

"It's impossible," she cried out, laughing so hard she ended up rolling on her back.

Meanwhile Gidi was sliding smoothly forward like a snake and reached the opposite wall in a few seconds.

"Way to go, Gids, mate!" called out Josh, and Becky gave him a lollipop as a prize. Gidi was so pleased he spent the rest of the evening with the lollipop in his mouth.

There were more games, even more wild and then Becky's dad called them all out into the garden for the last hour.

He'd lit a huge bonfire and they all had sparklers.

"Write your name in the air," Tamara said to Gidi.

"I did in Ivrit," said Gidi and grinned over at Becky.

Josh and Arthur helped to load marshmallows onto long sticks and everyone settled down on the grass to toast them.

The bonfire licked up into the clear frosty night. There was a full moon and as Tamara stared up she told herself, Bad things might be happening but when you've got your friends around you, they keep you safe against the dark. She caught Yaz's eye then and even though Yaz bumped shoulders with her, a tiny pang shot across Tamara's tummy as she remembered Yaz's words: Israel should stop now.

Why didn't she say anything about the hostages? How can Israel stop if the hostages aren't freed?

Then she gave herself a little shake.

Me and Yaz are solid, Tamara told herself. She won't stop being my friend because of this horrid war.

She bumped shoulders back, and Yaz let out a giggle.

Some people had crawled into their sleeping bags to keep out the cold and Gidi moaned his head was freezing.

"You wanted the haircut," said Tamara.

"*Ken,*" said Gidi, still with his lollipop in his mouth.

"*Ken and Barbie,*" shrieked Becky and Hannah.

"*Yoffe Toffee,*" Gidi shouted back above all the noise.

Tamara exchanged raised eyebrows with Yaz. "He's making jokes now."

"Proper settling in," said Yaz and they both reached out for another sparkler.

6

Miss Tate

Another week at school began and Tamara was sleeping better. She'd adjusted to the narrow chair bed and Eden was trying hard not to talk all the time. Sometimes they just lay on their beds, Tamara scrolling on her phone, Eden watching children's videos on Mum's tablet and when Tamara heard her little sister giggle at the cartoons, she smiled to herself. It made her feel quite grown up.

Tamara also loved her new desk in Mum and Dad's room. When she closed the door, it felt as though she was in a whole new world. Even better, when someone wanted her – Gidi, Eden, even Mum – they knocked on the door and waited until she called out, "Come in."

It made her feel like a Bank Manager or the Director of an IT company. Maybe that's what I'll do when I grow up, she thought.

Gidi was slow to get ready on Monday morning, grumbling about having to wear his uniform.

"Why do you wear so many clothes in England?" he moaned.

"To keep warm," said Mum.

"In Israel I wear T-shirt, shorts, trainers even in winter," Gidi muttered back, kicking his black leather shoes. "*Zeh lo noach* – it's uncomfortable."

Eden loved *zeh lo noach* and said it all the time, even in the wrong place.

"Your cereal can't be uncomfortable," said Tamara with a sigh at breakfast.

Gidi had his own locker now in school and kept it very tidy. Every morning, he hung up his coat and laid his baseball cap on the shelf. At lunchbreak he collected the cap and wore it until the bell went for lessons. He also wore it all the way to school and back.

Tamara said nothing. But just before Maths on Monday morning she'd grabbed Gidi's arm and said, "Don't put your pencils out – you know, like you do – until the teacher arrives. Then Dean won't swipe them on the floor. *Ken?*" She emphasized Ken, the Hebrew word for yes.

Gidi had ducked his head, but he'd nodded. He stopped putting out his pencils in all classes until a teacher arrived.

"At least no one notices anymore," Tamara had said to Yaz at lunch on Monday.

"Maybe it's helping him, you know, to get over it," Yaz had said.

But Tamara shook her head. She still felt as though it was her problem to solve. Gidi couldn't cope without his pencils. He wouldn't start work or even listen until they were set up.

He's dependent, like someone on drugs, she thought.

But she didn't feel she could say anything at home.

Tuesday morning started with Eden saying cereal *zeh lo noach* over and over until Tamara shouted at her to "Shut up!" Then Mum told Tamara off and Tamara stormed out to school, yelling at Gidi to keep up. But her temper had cooled by the time they reached the lockers and lessons started. Double Maths with Miss Tate.

Just get it out the way, Tamara told herself and then it was one of her favourite subjects, Geography with Miss Broome. "You'll like Geography," Tamara told Gidi as they sat down in Maths. "You can use all your pencils."

Gidi put his pencil case on the table, resting his hand on it as if for comfort.

Then Miss Tate swept in and shouted, "Sit. Quiet. Books open."

Today the teacher was wearing black trousers with knife-sharp creases down each leg, a black cardigan buttoned up with the collar of a white blouse over the rather severe neckline.

She looks like a policewoman, thought Tamara, and she drifted off into a daydream where the Head came in and said to Miss Tate, "Arrested anyone lately?"

A grin spread over Tamara's face without her realising it.

"Daydreaming again, Tamara Cohen. Demerit point. Homework book. Now."

Everyone craned round to stare.

Tamara went bright red and Gidi shuffled his chair forward to let her pass. He threw her an anxious look.

Tamara could feel her temper rising.

All I did was grin, she told herself, as she marched up to the front and flung her book down on the teacher's desk. But with a supreme effort she kept quiet. She couldn't risk being sent to the Head again. Fortunately, Miss Tate was distracted by a girl in the front row putting her hand up and asking a question. Without looking at Tamara, the teacher scribbled in the book and shoved it across the table back to her. Tamara swiped the book up, stuck her chin in the air, avoiding Lola's eye who was nudging Dean with a smirk, and went back to her seat.

For the rest of the lesson Tamara was too angry to listen, until a really hard question came up on the whiteboard. Almost instantly Gidi put his hand up. Tamara perked up, expecting Miss Tate to call on him. No one else put their hand up.

But Miss Tate ignored Gidi.

Tamara tapped her foot on the floor impatiently

while Gidi faced the front, his arm straight in the air. Miss Tate glared round the class for two whole minutes and then she barked out, "You should all know this one. Watch and learn."

The teacher tapped a few keys on the class computer and the solution appeared with no explanation.

"I don't get it," Tamara whispered to Gidi.

"Tell you later," whispered Gidi back, shooting a nervous glance towards the teacher.

Geography was the next lesson until lunch and there was no chance to meet up with Yaz and let off steam.

But this was a much more relaxed class with a newly qualified teacher, Miss Broome, a young woman in her early twenties who dyed her hair pink and wore skirts with cool tops or a jacket with the sleeves rolled up. Becky had asked once if the teacher liked Taylor Swift and Miss Broome had grinned and said, "Of course."

Tamara loved her class ever since.

Josh is right, she thought, as she sat next to Gidi again. Not all the teachers are like Miss Tate. Even Dad was right about meeting lots of new people in high school and not getting on with everyone. She suddenly longed to talk to Dad and explain that she knew she was wrong last Tuesday night and she was sorry and look how nice she was being to Gidi. But she didn't think he would listen.

The lesson was perfect for Gidi. Plenty of questions he could answer, the teacher was keen to pick him and there was a decent pie chart about climate change to fill in with his pencils. Once Gidi had completed the chart he took out a sharpener from the case, sharpened each pencil to a fine point again and lined them all up.

"How interesting," said Miss Broome. "I can see you're an organised person, Gideon."

But Gidi just sat there, with his arms folded, staring into space.

Tamara could see the teacher was puzzled. She felt a rush of hope. Maybe Miss Broome will sort out this pencil thing with Gidi.

But the teacher didn't say anything else and then the bell went.

Josh and Arthur collected Gidi for lunch and Yaz had a clarinet lesson. Miss Broome asked Tamara to help collect all the books.

By the time Tamara went into the corridor, there was no one around. They'd all rushed off to the lunch queue. It felt a bit spooky and Tamara realised it was the first time she'd been on her own since they started high school. For a second she wasn't sure which way to go. She walked to a corner and looked down the next long corridor. It was exactly the same as the last one. She was about to retrace her steps when she heard the harsh voice of Miss Tate. Peering back round the corner, Tamara could see Miss Broome in the doorway to her classroom, and Miss Tate was standing with her.

Miss Broome had a strained look on her face and Tamara stopped to listen in.

" . . . and all the suffering in Gaza," Miss Tate was saying.

Not more politics, thought Tamara, and was about to turn to go when Miss Broome started to speak. "Yes, it's awful, all the children suffering, on both sides," said Miss Broome in her gentle voice. She took a step back as Miss Tate leaned towards her.

Too close for comfort, thought Tamara.

"I should send you some links," said Miss Tate, her voice echoing the empty corridor. "Israel dropping all those bombs, killing children. And now we have to teach an Israeli child."

"Who's that?" said Miss Broome.

"Gideon Cohen, Tamara Cohen's cousin. His father is in the IDF, you know, the Israeli army. I'm not happy, not happy at all."

"He's only a child," said Miss Broome.

Miss Tate gave a snort. "Our Teachers' Union is organising a group to go to the march on Saturday," she said. "To protest about Israel bombing Gaza. Are you coming?"

Miss Broome looked quite flushed, Tamara thought, and then the younger teacher said in a quiet, but firm voice, "No, I don't think so."

"Pity," said Miss Tate. "But I can let you have a couple of badges, show solidarity. Like these." She unbuttoned her cardigan and Tamara could just make out the round shape of two badges pinned to the white shirt.

"Free Palestine," read out Miss Broome. "Global Intifada." Her voice sounded confused. "Are we allowed to wear those in school?"

"I keep them covered, so yes, that's fine," said the older teacher and then she strode off down the corridor.

In shock Tamara ran off, past all the Science rooms, round a corner and then she saw the double doors into the lunchroom up ahead. She ran on through the open doors and into the familiar hubbub of school with relief. Looking all around she found the others at a table. Yaz had joined them.

"My clarinet lesson was cancelled," she said, as Tamara sat down. "Did Miss Broome keep you back a long time?"

Tamara was out of breath and poured a cup of water.

Gidi, Josh and Arthur were all tucking into huge plates of spaghetti Bolognese.

"You won't believe what I saw," Tamara said, once she'd drunk a whole cup of water.

"Dean and Lola apologising," said Josh.

"What for?" asked Arthur, with his puzzled look.

"Existing," said Josh and they all laughed.

"Nothing like that," said Tamara and then as they listened wide eyed, she told them exactly what the two teachers had said.

"So, Miss Tate is angry about Gaza," said Yaz.

Tamara stared at her friend. "Yes. Seems so and she's told Miss Broome she doesn't want to teach an Israeli child."

Yaz didn't say anything.

But Arthur looked puzzled. "Who's she talking about?"

"Me," said Gidi in a small voice.

Tamara felt a chill go through her and she said, "Miss Tate hates Jews."

Doesn't Yaz get it? she thought, feeling confused.

"Well, she didn't actually say that, to be fair," said Yaz.

"She doesn't want to teach Gidi because he's Israeli. That's racist!" said Tamara, feeling her temper rise. "I'm going to go and find her and have a proper go this time. I don't care if I get expelled."

"Whoa," said Arthur. "You can't do that."

"Take it easy," said Josh, glancing over his shoulder.

"Lots of people are angry about Gaza," said Yaz in a voice a bit more cool than usual. "My cousin says Israel is killing a lot of women and children. They should stop."

Tamara looked at her with a jolt. Why is Yaz saying all this stuff? I thought she was on my side. What's going on?

But Yaz was picking bits of cucumber out of her baguette as if she had no idea what Tamara might be thinking. Tamara took a breath and then she said in a voice edged with anger, "So Israel should stop now even though Hamas has hundreds of hostages and no one knows anything about them, if they're alive or dead."

It was Yaz's turn to look confused and she dropped her eyes.

Come on, Yaz, Tamara pleaded silently. Don't you turn on me.

Then Yaz said in a voice which wobbled slightly, "I think my cousin has a point but I really don't understand much at all."

Tamara felt her insides fold inwards with disappointment.

Then Yaz spoke again and in her more normal voice. "Whatever, it doesn't excuse Miss Tate taking it out on Gidi or the Jewish kids in our school. That's not right."

Tamara felt a little pulse of relief. "OK," she said.

"My dad says not all Muslims feel the same about the war," said Yaz.

Tamara could see her friend was looking confused again.

"Jews have different opinions too about the war," said Josh. "That's what my dad says."

"My mum and I don't watch the news," said Arthur, with a shrug.

"It's important to watch," said Yaz. "We watch the news with Mum and Dad and discuss what's happening. If you want to have an opinion, you have to be informed."

"My gran says there's so much fake news and propaganda," said Tamara.

She hoped that Yaz would agree with her. But her friend just shrugged.

So, what does that mean? thought Tamara.

"It's OK to watch news and stuff," said Josh. "But Mum says people have become obsessed with the Israel/Gaza war and taking sides and marching and stuff. What about all the other bad things going on in the world, like war in Ukraine and famine in Sudan?"

"Exactly," cried out Tamara. "And now Miss Tate is trying to get Miss Broome on her side. It's only going to get worse in school. We have to do something."

They were quiet for a few moments and then Yaz said, "Look, I agree, Miss Tate can't get away with picking on the Jewish kids. That's racist. What can we do?"

Tamara found herself feeling almost pathetically grateful that her best friend had finally said something supportive. But why can't I count on her, like normal? she couldn't help wondering. We always agree on everything but suddenly there's like a big gap opening up between us. Does Yaz feel it too or is it just me?

A lonely feeling swept through Tamara while everyone stayed silent.

Then Arthur spoke up. "In football, if someone fouls me deliberately, I don't go and run him down and kick him back. I wait for the right opportunity and then I outwit him, grab the ball and score. Makes him look a right idiot."

Yaz clicked her fingers. "That's it!" she said. "We outwit Miss Tate and I think I've got an idea."

Once she'd told them they could hardly wait for the Maths class on Wednesday morning.

As Miss Tate entered class the next morning, everyone was sitting down except Tamara and Yaz, who rushed in behind her.

"Sorry we're late, Miss," said Yaz. "Someone told us to bring you this glass of water."

Miss Tate turned on her heel and opened her mouth to bark at the girls when Yaz arrived at the desk, came to an abrupt halt and Tamara crashed into her back. The huge glass of water spilled all over Miss Tate's bright yellow cardigan.

"You clumsy girl!" shrieked Miss Tate.

She tried to brush the water off but the cardigan was soaked and in the end she unbuttoned it and threw it on a chair.

"Free Palestine!" cried out Dean, pointing to the large badge on Miss Tate's shirt.

"Global Intifada!" yelled Lola, and she and Dean began to shout out both the slogans. Some of the others joined in and the class were in an uproar.

This is a disaster, thought Tamara almost in tears. Gidi already had his pencils laid out and he was sitting even more rigid than normal.

I've messed up, I'm such an idiot, she told herself.

Suddenly a voice boomed from the doorway, "Silence!"

It was Mrs Cole, the Head.

7
Spotlight Club

Tamara's eyes locked with Yaz and they both froze. There was the shuffling of feet as the class threw themselves into their seats. Dean and Lola exchanged smirks and for a second Tamara felt her temper rise. But Yaz grabbed her arm and pulled her down onto a seat next to Gidi.

Miss Tate was the first to break the silence. "That stupid girl has soaked my blouse."

But Mrs Cole was glaring round the room.

Satisfied that the class were under her full control, she directed her gaze at Miss Tate. "I see," said Mrs Cole. And then she seemed to do a double take as she looked at Miss Tate and her wet blouse. She's seen the badges, thought Tamara. But will she care? Does she understand what they mean?

Gran had been very clear last Friday night.

"When the marchers shout Global Intifada they

mean, attack Jewish people all over the world. Many of the marchers might not understand and they're not all anti-Semitic, but there's plenty of agitators who are being racist. We've heard them shout out things against Jews, me, Maurice and the Lunch Bunch. So, what are we going to do about it? That's the question for Jews today."

"But pensioners and children aren't going to sort it," Mum had said.

"Everyone has to do their bit," said Gran and then Mum changed the subject, quizzing Gidi and Tamara about their schoolwork.

Tamara had no idea what they should do or how she could do her bit, as Gran said.

Now, as she stared at the Head, she had a sinking feeling in her stomach.

What if Mrs Cole thinks the badges are OK? She might even tell all the teachers to wear badges like that. But before her thoughts could get any worse, Mrs Cole said in a firm voice, "Miss Tate, please come to my office after this lesson."

Tamara swivelled round to catch Yaz's eye and gave her a questioning look. Yaz shrugged back.

Miss Tate gave Mrs Cole her coldest stare and said, "Of course."

Then she turned to the class and barked, "Page 11. Complete. In Silence. Now!"

It was PE before lunch and then they all met in the

lunchroom. Becky and Hannah joined their table too. Everyone started talking at once. Even Gidi looked interested. Will Miss Tate get the sack? Will all the teachers start wearing badges? Then Becky said, "Listen up! I know what happened."

They all stopped and looked at Becky.

"So, two girls in Y8 I know heard everything the Head said."

"How?" said Arthur.

"They were sitting outside the door when Miss Tate went in and she didn't shut the door properly," said Becky.

"Miss Tate never could keep her voice down," said Josh and he bumped fists with Arthur.

"So," went on Becky, "they heard Miss Tate getting a right telling off. She's not allowed to wear any badges like that ever again. The teachers aren't allowed to take sides in school, not politics or anything, Mrs Cole said. My friends didn't understand it all but when Miss Tate came out, she looked proper angry."

"The plan worked," said Arthur. "Like I said in football. Don't get mad. Get even."

"High five!" cried out Josh and they all slapped palms around the group.

As the others chattered on laughing and making jokes, all Tamara could feel was relief that she hadn't let Gidi down after all. From now on, she told herself, I'm going to be the best-behaved kid in the year and just look after my cousin. No more trouble.

There was a lull as everyone ate some lunch.

Then Josh said, "Gidi, why did you get taken out of PE?"

"What?" said Tamara, feeling alarmed again.

"Mrs Cole has put me into Z Group for Maths," said Gidi in a quiet voice.

"Wow!" said Josh. "You're a genius, then. That's for the gifted kids."

"*Sabab*," said Gidi. "Awesome. I'll take my pencil case," and he shot a look towards Tamara. She rolled her eyes back and for a moment she and Gidi were actually grinning about those silly pencils. At least he won't be with Miss Tate anymore, she told herself. Z Group had the marvellous Mr Mackie who was serious, kind and could be a lot of fun. Do Mum and Dad know Gidi is a genius? she couldn't help wondering.

Josh was speaking again. "Coming to Spotlight Club tonight, Gidi?"

"What's that?" asked Gidi, picking up his last slice of pizza.

"We go Wednesday nights. You can do five-a-side football, drama . . . um . . ."

"Dance," said Becky.

"I don't do dance," said Gidi.

Tamara bumped shoulders with him, "Neither do we. Yaz does Arts and Crafts, Hannah and me do drama and there's chess."

Gidi brightened up. "I love chess. Me and Yussuf play."

"Sorted," said Arthur. "I have football training instead. Tell me all about it tomorrow."

As they walked home after school, Tamara said to Gidi, "Pick up speed, cuz, there's a lot to do."

Gidi had started to walk properly instead of shuffle to and from school, but Tamara was in a hurry. Wednesday evenings were always a rush.

"We have to get home and change for Club," she went on, a bit breathless now as they strode along, Gidi keeping up with her for once. "Then homework. Mum makes dinner for us and Eden at five thirty. Yaz's mum picks us up at six and drives us to Club."

"*Yoffee Toffee*," puffed out Gidi.

Tamara looked round at him and bumped shoulders so hard Gidi nearly lost his balance. They burst into laughter and broke into a run for the last few metres, arriving at the front door red faced and breathing hard.

As they went into the hall, Mum appeared in a floury apron. "You two sound jolly," she said, with a bright smile.

"Gidi's in Z class for Maths now," cried out Tamara. "Did you know he's a genius?"

Gidi dropped his school bag, slipped out of his coat and hung it up on a peg.

Mum was wiping her hands on her apron and when Gidi turned, his cheeks still quite rosy, she said, "Your abba said you were clever, darling. He's been worried you might be overlooked in a London school."

Gidi ducked his head and didn't say anything.

He's very modest, thought Tamara. He could have done a big show off at lunch in front of Arthur and Josh about his gifted class. A warm feeling went through her and she said to Mum, "Gidi's going to do brilliantly. You'll see."

Then she and Gidi took their schoolbags and went upstairs to do homework.

Tamara changed into jeans and a clean top, went into Mum's room and switched on her laptop. There was a gentle knock at the door and Mum put her head into the room. "I'm so proud of you, Tamara. Gidi's settling down and you've really helped. Well done."

Tamara blushed a deep red.

Then Mum added before she disappeared, "I'm driving you to Club tonight. Yaz's mum is picking up Kadija."

Mum disappeared.

Tamara felt that tiny pang in her tummy again. So Yaz is going to Club with her cousin, who is filling her head with stuff about Israel and Gaza. Are me and Yaz still best friends? she wondered.

On time, Gidi was downstairs in jeans, a sweatshirt and the inevitable baseball cap, ready for dinner. Eden talked non-stop at dinner, but Gidi smiled a lot and nodded. Then all three went out to the car and Mum dropped Gidi and Tamara at the Spotlight Club. Their friends had already arrived.

"Over here, Gids," Josh called out and Tamara watched as Josh waved to the chess tables. Gidi went over and sat down with a group of boys and girls setting out the boards.

Tamara looked round for Yaz and saw her in the Arts and Crafts area, sitting at a table with Kadija and a couple of other Muslim girls, who wore bright headscarves.

Her mood started to dip and then Hannah called her over to the drama group.

Tamara had always loved Wednesday nights. She had to miss last week because Gidi was arriving. And I was furious, she remembered. But it's better now, even if he drives me crazy sometimes.

"What are we doing?" she called out to Josie, the youth leader.

"OK," said Josie in a loud voice, "listen up."

The drama group settled down.

"Groups of four. Five props each from the basket." Josie pointed to a large wicker basket against the wall. "Make up a story using all five props. Who are your characters? What's the problem? Think of the ups and downs in your story. How will it end?"

"I love this one," said Hannah, grabbing Tamara's arm.

They joined up with two boys, Jermaine and Zak, and rushed over to the wicker basket. Between them they grabbed an old mobile phone, a wooden spoon, an orange, a pair of shorts for a toddler and a whistle.

"I wanted that calculator," whined Hannah. "Someone nabbed it."

"But we got the phone," said Tamara. "How about a robbery? The toddler's baking with Mum." She held up the wooden spoon with a grin. "A burglar bursts in, the toddler grabs the phone, mum chucks the orange at the burglar but he ducks . . ."

" . . . and then the burglar ties Mum up," went on Hannah, "and starts to stuff all the jewellery in a big bag and . . . and . . ."

" . . . but the toddler has pressed 999 by mistake and just as the burglar runs off, the police arrive," cut in Zak.

"Cool," said Jermaine, the fourth member of their group. "I'm the burglar."

"I'll be the toddler," said Zak. He picked up the shorts and pulled them over his head.

"Idiot," said Tamara with a grin. "I'll be the mum."

She grabbed the spoon and put the orange on the floor.

"Hannah, you be the police."

"I need the whistle," said Hannah.

Tamara tossed it over.

They had less than ten minutes left to create their story, and they nearly didn't finish because the boys started to toss the orange between them and then play cricket with their hands as bats. Hannah had a call on her phone and settled into a long chat until Tamara frowned at her. Meanwhile, the music from the dance group at the other end of the hall was deafening.

Finally, Josie called them all together. The dance music was turned down and when Tamara looked around, she saw Gidi bent over a chess board, concentrating on the next move from a girl opposite Tamara hadn't seen before. The girl wore a green headscarf and had a look of deep concentration on her face.

Gidi's OK, she told herself and then it was the turn of her group to show their play.

Everyone laughed a lot and clapped wildly.

A rush of happiness welled up through Tamara and she waved to Becky across the room in the dance group.

At break there was fruit, crisps, chocolate bars and cola.

Tamara went over to join Gidi and the chess group. Gidi had an apple in one hand and a chocolate bar in another. He was standing near to the chess girl. Neither of them was speaking.

"Who won?" said Tamara in a bright voice.

I sound like Mum, she couldn't help thinking.

"Me," said Gidi, swallowing some chocolate. "But Selma's good."

He nodded to the girl in the green hijab.

"County chess champion three years running," said Selma, not meeting Tamara's eyes. "Gidi's very good. Should enter next time."

"When?" said Gidi.

"May. Next year."

Gidi shrugged and Tamara could almost read his mind.

He doesn't want to be here for months, she told herself. Why would he? He wants to go home.

It made her feel sad but then Gidi broke into her thoughts, as some of the others came over.

"It's like my club here," he said, as he finished off his snacks.

"Where's that?" said Jermaine.

"My club in Haifa," said Gidi.

Jermaine shrugged.

"In Israel," explained Gidi. "I go to a club called Pomegranates for Peace. We all meet up and I play chess with my best friend, Yussuf."

"Israel?" said Jermaine in a tight voice.

"Yussuf?" said Zak. "That's a Muslim name."

Tamara felt herself tense and a flicker of red-hot chilli rise up in her. Do I always have to be ready now to stand up for Gidi? Because we're Jewish and he's from Israel. Ridiculous!

She looked round for Yaz, but her friend was standing by the snacks table with Kadija and the other Muslim girls. The little group were in a huddle and suddenly Kadija looked over her shoulder, stared right at Tamara and then turned back and whispered something behind her hand to Yaz. Yaz shrugged but she didn't look round. Tamara suddenly felt so alone, as if she no longer fitted in anywhere. Why would Yaz do that? thundered through her head and she felt tears prick in her eyes.

But Gidi was speaking again and Tamara tuned back in.

"I'm Jewish and Yussuf is Muslim," Gidi was saying. "We live in the same apartment building, on different floors. We go to our club together on Tuesday nights."

"Nah," said Jermaine. "That's rubbish. Israel's evil. They kill Muslims, they don't play chess with them."

Gidi shook his head in his quiet but firm way while Jermaine glared at him. No one else spoke up and Tamara felt as though her voice had disappeared. If I say anything, she thought, Yaz and her cousin might hear and what if they laugh at me?

She couldn't bear it.

But then she remembered Gran and the Lunch Bunch, standing up for Jewish people in Trafalgar Square and a little bit of red-hot chilli pushed down the fear. This is my chance to do something, she told herself, whatever Yaz or anyone else thinks.

In a voice which trembled slightly, Tamara said, "My gran says there is right and wrong on both sides. But Jews and Muslims can be friends."

She looked over at Selma, the chess girl. Selma looked younger than Tamara and her friends. More like Gidi, Tamara decided. But the other girl gave a firm nod and without meeting anyone's eyes as usual, she said, "Yes. Gidi is my chess friend."

"Like me and Yussuf," said Gidi. "Our *madrichim* . . ."

" . . . mad what?" butted in Jermaine.

"*Madrichim*. It means youth club leaders, like Josie," said Gidi. "Our *madrichim*, Omer and Farrah, run the club for Jews and Muslims, all together for peace. Omer is Jewish and Farrah is Muslim but they're best friends."

"Weird," said Jermaine. "That's not what everyone says on the socials."

"My gran says you have to check all your facts to find out what is true," said Tamara, feeling bolder now that Gidi was speaking up.

"Yussuf's dad is an Israeli border guard on the Gaza border right now," Gidi went on. "He's helping to keep everyone in Israel safe. And they have family in Gaza. They're very worried about them. My dad's an army medic in the south. The bombing and the war is scary for everyone. We were in the bomb shelters together, Yussuf's family and mine and all the people in our building. Scared, together . . ." Gidi face flushed and his voice tailed off.

They all stood in silence for a moment.

Then Jermaine broke the silence. "Me and Zak, we don't know all that stuff." He gave Zak a nod.

But Zak went red and couldn't meet Jermaine's eye.

Tamara had seen the two boys together at school, but she didn't really know them. They seemed to be glued to screens at breaktime, playing computer games together.

Now Zak said, "I do know that stuff. Only I don't talk about it."

"What do you mean?" said Jermaine, giving him a curious look.

Zak pulled a small blue cap out of his pocket.

It's a kippa, thought Tamara in surprise.

"I'm Jewish," said Zak in a nervous voice and he put the kippa on his head. "I'm too scared to tell anyone at school. Mum has cousins in Israel and one of them was at the dance festival when the terrorists came. She managed to hide and escape but Mum still bursts into tears when the news comes on."

"I didn't know," said Jermaine.

"Sorry," muttered Zak. "It's only me and Mum and she's afraid we'll be attacked in the street if we look Jewish."

"I can't hide being black," said Jermaine, in a low voice.

"I know. Racism's not fair," declared Zak.

There was a silence and then Zak said, "Still friends?" He gave Jermaine an anxious look.

"Course," said Jermaine, crinkling his eyes. "Who else can I smash at Minecraft?"

That made them laugh and Tamara felt a bit less tense.

Then Josh said, "So in your club, Gids, do you talk about politics and stuff all the time?"

"*Ma Pitom!* No way!" said Gidi. "We're sick of the news. In Club we just hang up."

That did it. Everyone burst into shrieks of laughter and shouted back, "Out! Hang out, Gidi."

Gidi laughed out loud too and then he said, "*Yoffe Toffee.*"

And even though most people didn't understand they all started to say, *Yoffee Toffee.*

"Good night out?" Mum asked when they arrived home.

"*Yoffee Toffee,*" said Gidi.

Tamara just gave a nod.

"Lovely," said Mum. "Up you go, you both look shattered."

As Tamara kissed the sleeping Eden good night and climbed into bed half an hour later, she thought, I'm glad Gidi spoke up about Jews and Muslims. And why didn't I know Zak is Jewish? I'm glad Jermaine and Zak are still friends.

But what about me and Yaz?

8

Family Outing

"Family outing tomorrow," Dad announced at Saturday lunch. "Make sure you get all your homework done today."

"Can we buy friendship bracelets, please, Daddy?" said Eden.

Dad gave Eden a smile and said, "Perhaps."

Then Mum said in her quiet voice, "I must tell you, Ben, that Tamara has really helped Gidi to settle in. And the school have put him in the gifted set for Maths. Did you know Gidi was gifted?"

Dad flushed slightly and then he said, "Yes, of course. David told me but we've been so busy, I didn't have a chance to ring the school."

That's so patronising, thought Tamara.

She hardly recognised good old Dad these days. He's no fun anymore, she told herself with an inward sigh.

"Anyway, well done, Gidi," Dad went on.

There was an awkward silence while everyone waited for Dad to praise Tamara.

But he didn't and so Mum said, "And well done, Tamara."

Dad picked up his fork, gave a slight nod and said in a cool voice, "Yes, well, only what I expect from you, Tamara."

That did it. Chilli flowing through her veins as if she'd swallowed the fiery red peppers whole, Tamara pushed back her chair and shouted out, "I'm done!"

"But what about dessert?" wailed Eden and she put her thumb in her mouth.

Tamara looked down at little Eden with her sad face close to tears. Don't Mum and Dad care about her? she thought. All this tension. She's only six.

Even Gidi looked upset.

I bet he's dying to get those flipping pencils out, she told herself.

She gave a sigh and said, "Don't want dessert."

Then she ran off upstairs to Mum and Dad's room and threw herself down at her desk.

She'd pinned a new Taylor Swift postcard to her noticeboard this week, about building bridges when someone upsets you. Now as she stared at it, she murmured aloud, "It's hopeless. Dad and me, we're never gonna build a bridge. I feel like I've got 100 demerit points."

The rest of the day passed for Tamara under a

gloomy cloud. There was radio silence from Yaz, not a message or a funny pic or anything. That was so unusual and after everything this week and Yaz choosing to sit with her cousin at lunch every day, Tamara didn't feel she could send a message. We're not absolute best friends anymore, she told herself, tears welling in her eyes.

After lunch she asked Gidi if he wanted to walk up to the shops.

But he shook his head and said, "Have to catch up with the Maths set. I don't want to lose my place."

Eden had a play date, so there was no one to hang out with.

Tamara stayed upstairs, finishing all her homework, including most of the half term History project, way before the deadline. There was nothing else to do.

As she settled down to sleep that night she wondered if Dad would loosen up on the outing tomorrow. Tamara loved family outings, but there was none of the excitement fizzing inside her this time.

Sunday dawned bright and sunny but rather cold.

Mum made a cooked breakfast. "I remember your mum telling me your appetite went through the roof this year, Gidi, darling," she said, as she plopped another fried egg onto the boy's plate.

Gidi muttered, "Thank you."

Bet he's missing his mum, Tamara thought, shooting Gidi a sympathetic smile. I've never been away from home for nearly two weeks, like Gidi.

Tamara decided to make an extra effort to cheer Gidi up and this included keeping away from Dad so that they didn't clash again.

She took Eden's hand in the street, once they all left the house, to show how responsible she could be, and kept up a cheerful patter to Gidi. "Eden wants to go to the Shard, don't you, Eden?"

"Yes," said Eden. "It's got 32,000 floors and you need 20 lifts to get up into the sky."

Tamara rolled her eyes at Gidi and he grinned back.

"Actually, it's got 72 floors," said Tamara, "and you can see for 40 miles all around London. But I think Dad wants to go to St Paul's Cathedral."

"We went there last time we were in London," said Gidi in a bored voice. "Keren spent most of her time on her phone."

"I remember," said Tamara.

She was dying to banter with Dad about the outing; where they were going, what they'd eat, but she didn't dare speak to him.

If we have a row on the Underground, it'll spoil the whole day, she thought, with a prickly feeling inside her.

Once they were on the platform, Dad said, "Right, we're going to London Bridge. I've booked tickets for the Shard . . ."

Eden cut in with an ear-splitting squeal and began springing up and down on her toes. "You're the best most wonderfullest daddy in the whole world!" she cried out and everyone laughed.

Gidi's face split into a grin. "*Yoffee toffee*," he said and bumped shoulders with Tamara.

"OK, calm down you lot," said Dad and Tamara spotted something of the old fun Dad. "Then we'll go to Borough Market for lunch."

"Hooray," cheered Tamara and Eden together.

"There's the hugest food there," said Eden. "Even enough for you, Gidsy."

"Awesome," said Gidi and they all laughed again as the train rumbled into the station.

Tamara and Gidi, with Eden between them, sat on the opposite side to Mum and Dad, but further down the carriage. It felt as though they were travelling alone and Eden started to imagine they were going to Africa to see the elephants.

"Or Greenland," said Gidi.

"Why Greenland?" said Tamara.

"To see how the Inuits live. I've never seen much snow, only once in Jerusalem for a few hours. I'd like to build an igloo."

"You'd freeze," said Eden.

"Not if you gave me your gloves," said Gidi in a teasing voice.

"You've got your own," said Eden with a frown.

"I'm from Israel where it's hot. I need your gloves and mine and Tamara's and . . ."

" . . . A hundred gloves?"

"*Ken,*" said Gidi.

But Tamara could see Eden was tired with the noise and stuffiness on the train. She drew the little girl onto her lap and Eden rested her head against her sister's shoulder.

Tamara heard Gidi let out a sigh.

"What's up?" she said.

"It would be great if Keren was here."

They stared at each other in silence, Tamara giving a small nod to show she understood Gidi was missing his sister. Then Eden climbed off Tamara's lap and onto Gidi's thin legs. He closed his arms around her waist and leaned his cheek against her head. They stayed like that all the way to London Bridge station, when Dad came over and, taking Eden's hand, said, "Come on, this is our stop."

It was wonderful to be out in the fresh air again. As they arrived on the street, there was the Shard rising into the sky so high they all had to crick their necks to see the top. Dad led the way to the entrance. They joined a queue to show their tickets and then another queue for the lift.

"But it'll be worth the wait," said Tamara, as Eden jiggled with impatience around their feet.

"72 floors," said Gidi. "I've never been so high."

"Me neither. We can take selfies and send them to Keren," said Tamara and that made Gidi smile.

Finally, it was their turn for the lift and once they

were inside, they seemed to shoot upwards, which was a bit scary. Tamara was glad when the doors opened on the 72nd floor.

Only nothing in the whole of her life had prepared her for this!

As they stepped out, cold air whirled around them, making Tamara shiver. She zipped up her jacket and then, copying Mum and Dad, she looked up, but all she could see was sky which went on and on. Tamara began to feel quite dizzy. But worse, much worse, when she looked forward, there were no walls keeping them in and safe. Instead, there were just huge glass panels, from floor to ceiling. Through the glass, the whole world opened out. A funny feeling spread through Tamara and she flattened herself against the solid wall, next to the lift. Her knees began to shake.

"Come on, Gidsy!" cried out Eden and grabbing her cousin's hand, they raced over to the view.

Hands and faces pressed hard into the glass wall, they started to shout and point out the famous sights of London.

"We're higher than a mountain," yelled Eden. "It's amazingly amazing!"

"That's St Paul's Cathedral, isn't it, Aunty Mel?" said Gidi, his nose pressed flat to the glass.

"Yes, well done, Gidi," said Mum. "And over there, that white arch, that's Wembley Stadium, home to English football."

"Awesome," said Gidi.

Eden slapped the glass and cried out, "That's the bridge that opens, Mummy, look over there."

"Tower Bridge," said Mum, "and the Tower of London next to it."

"Where?" said Gidi, twisting his neck.

"That old-looking castle on the river," said Mum.

"I see it, I see it!!" said Eden in her high-pitched, over-excited voice."

Tamara could see it too, but nothing would make her walk towards that terrifying glass wall.

"Everything looks like my toys," Eden said, staring down. "Look, Mummy, a tiny church and that building over there, all glass but so tiny. I wish I could pick them up and play with them."

"Just like toys," agreed Gidi.

Dad strolled towards over to the group and Tamara felt a pang that she was too scared to enjoy the views. But she noticed that Dad stood quite a few feet away from the glass wall. He was scrolling endlessly on his phone, which irritated Tamara.

"Come on, Tamsy!" cried out Eden, waving a hand towards her sister.

Gidi had a puzzled look on his face as he stared over.

But all Tamara could do was shake her head, her throat closed in fear.

It's too scary, she thought. I'm not moving. What if the wall collapsed and we fell? It's 1,016 feet all the way down to the ground. If I went over the edge, no one could save me.

The thought made her feel so dizzy, she dropped down onto the floor and bent her head.

When Tamara looked up again, she spotted Dad sitting on a bar stool, with a coffee in front of him, talking on his phone. Can't he even be with us on a family outing? she told herself. Does he have to talk to everyone about the war all day, every day? Her chilli temper threatened to rise. It's so unfair to poor Gidi, she wanted to shout to Dad. This is his first family outing and Dad's ignoring him. Then she saw Mum, Eden and Gidi, arriving back. Eden ran over to Tamara. "Isn't it the bestest view in the whole world?"

Tamara forced a grin and said, "You bet it is. Toilet?"

Eden nodded.

With relief at the thought of escaping for a few minutes, Tamara called over to Mum, "We're going to the loo."

Mum gave her a nod. Dad didn't look up. Gidi had climbed up on a bar stool and was tapping on his phone too.

Messaging Keren, thought Tamara, as she took Eden's hand and headed for the lift.

They had to go down to floor sixty-eight and Tamara decided she'd never felt so safe in her all her life as she did inside the solid walls of the lift. She wished she could stay there all the way back to the street, but she knew Mum would be furious if she disappeared with Eden.

As they left the lift, Eden said, "This way."

They walked towards the sign and pushed open a door.

"No way!" Tamara cried out, as her head spun.

The cubicle was so tiny they were almost pressed up against the outside wall. Only it was floor to ceiling glass with an almost transparent blind over it. Then Eden pressed a button on the wall and the blind flew up. The Thames spread out three hundred metres beneath them, as clear as day. Tamara felt her stomach turn over and she nearly threw up in the sink.

"Look at all the toy boats on the river," said Eden, her nose pressed to the glass. "I can wee and look at them all at the same time.

Chattering away in a bright voice, Eden sat down on the toilet.

Tamara decided it was the longest wee in history. Her sister kept on talking about everything she could see for miles and miles. Tamara thought she'd never shut up.

In the end, Tamara said, "I'll give you three friendship bracelets if you just finish up."

That did it. Eden jumped off, washed her hands and was out of the door, Tamara grabbing her hand before she reached the lift.

They went back up to the top floor. Mum was standing near Gidi, but Dad was still on his bar stool, head bent, ignoring everyone, scrolling on his phone. It was as if something snapped in Tamara and, striding over, she said, "Can't you take your eyes off your phone for one minute! I thought this was a family day out."

Dad looked up and for a second his eyes were glazed over. Then he seemed to snap to attention and fixing Tamara with his new, quite horrid glare, he started up in one long stream. "That's typical of you, Tamara, as usual only thinking of yourself. I'm on the phone to Uncle David with all our news from London and he's worried about Gidi and Keren and Aunty Sharon, you're so selfish . . ."

"Whaaat!!" interrupted Tamara, in full chilli temper mode now. "You're the selfish one! You don't care about any of us. The only way you'd pay us any attention is if we went to live in Israel!"

There was a shocked silence, and some people walked past giving them strange looks.

Tamara was mortified. Now everyone knows our business, she thought and these days she didn't even know if it was safe to say the word Israel aloud in public.

"Eden, Gidi, go to the lift, please, and wait for us. Ben, put that phone away, and Tamara, come this way, please." Mum handed out instructions in her firm, quiet voice and even Dad did what he was told.

Tamara was on the edge of tears as she followed Mum to the wall next to the lift. "It's so unfair, Mum.

It's like there's one rule for Dad these days and one for the rest of us."

"I know, darling," said Mum in a comforting voice. "But you've let off steam now. Can you try to get through lunch?"

Tamara gave a sullen shrug.

Mum nodded in a weary way and then she went over to Eden and Gidi and pressed the lift button. Dad joined them but Tamara hung back. In the last few seconds before the lift closed on them, Tamara stepped out.

"See you on the street," she called out before the doors closed.

Mum gave her a grave nod and Tamara felt herself beginning to calm down.

9

Football Game

By the time they arrived home on Sunday afternoon, Tamara had to admit that the day had turned out OK after all. Gidi had had eaten a giant burger which even Dad joked about. "Bigger than your head, mate."

Eden was in heaven when they'd found an entire stall devoted to friendship bracelets and Tamara bought her three, as she'd promised. Mum had left Gidi and Eden with Dad for half an hour, "while the ladies go for coffee," she'd said, with a wink to Tamara.

Feeling very grown up, Tamara had chosen a cappuccino with a perfect heart shape drawn in the froth by the barista and a slice of chocolate cake. It was lovely to chill out with Mum and gossip about all the fashions as people walked past.

In bed that night, Tamara decided that Dad was so much more relaxed once they'd left the Shard. Just like me, she realised. Then she had a funny thought.

Dad didn't go near those glass walls either. Is that why he sat on the bar stool? Was he scared too?

"We're like two peas in a pod," Dad always told her when she was little. It made her feel warm and fuzzy all over.

Me and Dad, went through her head now. Me and Dad were both afraid at the top of the Shard. That's why he sat as far away from the glass as possible, scrolling on his phone.

If the right moment comes, I'll ask him, she told herself before she fell asleep.

The school week started quite well. Gidi was much happier in his new Maths class and Tamara felt she was being successful at keeping her chilli temper under control. Even in Miss Tate's classes. Yaz still kept her distance but at least there weren't any more remarks about Israel and Gaza. Tamara often felt that strange, lonely feeling as she went round school without her best friend by her side.

But my job, she told herself with a grim determination, is to make sure there are no more problems for Gidi.

One good thing: Dean and Lola seemed to have lost interest in Gidi and his Israeli baseball cap. The pencil case was still a problem, but Tamara found she noticed the obsessive line up much less because Gidi didn't get his pencils out until the whole class was sitting down. The geography teacher continued to praise him for being well organised and Tamara had begun to wonder if Yaz had got it wrong, comparing Gidi to the woman who washed her hands thirty times a day because she was stressed.

She could have asked Yaz of course and then they would sit on a bench outside and spend lunch break chatting, like they used to. But that was before, she told herself, sadness welling up inside her. Yaz went round at lunch break with Kadjia and her crowd now.

It rained all day Monday and the whole school became edgy, stuffed up indoors. Then Tuesday dawned dry but overcast.

"Let's go outside and start a game," said Arthur as the boys bolted down pizzas in the lunchroom. He went off to collect his ball.

Tamara was sitting with Becky and Hannah at lunch.

Yaz wasn't around and Tamara felt very aware of her old friend's absence. Sometimes they caught each other's eyes in the corridor and Tamara would smile. Yaz usually smiled back but that was all.

Now Tamara strolled outside, arm in arm with Becky and Hannah. They settled on the picnic benches, putting down plastic bags to keep out the damp. Becky and Hannah started to sing a Taylor Swift song and Tamara joined in, as they leaned their heads together.

Out of the corner of her eye, Tamara could see Gidi sitting on another bench with Selma, the chess girl from Club and they had a small chess set between them. Selma was wearing the navy-blue hijab which was part of school uniform and her forehead was furrowed in a deep frown. Selma is Muslim, Tamara couldn't help thinking. But she's happy to be friends with Gidi. So, what happened between me and Yaz? But her mind was tired from turning the same thing over and over.

The song finished and above the hubbub a voice called out, "Football game, mate?"

It was Dean, and he was nodding towards Arthur, who still had his ball under his arm.

Something tightened in Tamara's chest which was strange. It's only the boys organising football, she told herself, but she couldn't help wondering, Why's Dean asking Arthur for a game?

"OK, two teams," Dean was saying. "I'll pick and Josh picks."

Tamara slid off the bench, that tight feeling still across her chest and walked towards the boys. She hadn't joined in with football since primary school. But something was different today. She heard Becky call her back but she didn't turn.

Hannah appeared at Tamara's side, a puzzled frown on her face. Hannah was in the girl's football team and Tamara enjoyed all sports, but Becky hated running around. Tamara knew she would stay on the picnic bench. Yaz wouldn't join in either but Tamara didn't turn round to search for her old friend. Becky can keep an eye on Gidi for me, Tamara thought and then wondered why she was worried anyway.

Dean picked Lola and Jermaine, as well as several other boys and girls. Zak shook his head when Jermaine called him over and went to sit out. Dean's team lined up opposite Josh's team, which included Arthur, Tamara, Hannah and some others.

This is going to be a tough game, thought Tamara, with Dean and Arthur up against each other. But why does Dean want this and why has Lola joined in? I've never seen Lola play football before, she told herself.

Lola was big and very strong. With broad shoulders, wide thighs and strong arms, Lola shoved her way around the school, swiping away other kids. In the corridors, space opened up to avoid an elbow in the ribs, or a kick on the ankle.

Tamara focused back on the game. The two teams were ready and then Dean pointed towards Josh's team and called out, "You're Israel and we're Palestine."

A jeer went up from Lola and some of the others around her joined in but before anyone could object, Dean slapped the ball out of Arthur's arms and kicked it towards the goal end. It veered right but Jermaine caught it and slammed it into the back of the net.

"Palestine: 1. Israel: nil. Yaay!" cried out Lola.

Arthur and Josh exchanged angry looks and then before Dean's team could regroup, Arthur caught the ball on his magical right foot, passed it to Josh, they both ran forward, Josh passed it back and Arthur volleyed it into the net.

Catching the ball on the rebound, Arthur held it firmly to his chest and walked to the centre of the pitch.

"Let's get this game started properly," he said, in his mild voice.

Dean walked over and stood opposite Arthur. "This is gonna be a massacre, Israel," he mocked.

"We didn't agree to those team names. It's so stupid," called out Josh.

"Shut up, Israel," called back Jermaine and he and Lola high fived.

"Let's just play," said Arthur. "It's one all and there's five minutes to the bell."

He tossed the ball up, Dean shouldered him out of the way and caught the ball on his foot. He kicked it towards Lola, then Hannah intercepted and dribbled forward, passing to Josh. But Lola stuck out her foot and Hannah tripped, ending up on the ground.

"Ow! My knee!" cried out Hannah.

Dean laughed out loud, grabbed Josh's shirt, stole the ball, and with a powerful swing of his right leg, slammed the ball into the net again.

With a whoop, Lola yelled out, "Palestine: 2. Now, Dean!"

Puffed out from chasing the ball, Tamara had bent to catch her breath. As she straightened, she saw Dean and Lola pull out long black and white checked scarves called keffiyehs, from under their school sweaters. Dean and Lola wrapped the scarves around their heads and then covered their eyes with sunglasses.

OMG! thought Tamara in horror. They look just like those protesters who surrounded Gran and the Lunch Bunch at Trafalgar Square, on the march.

She'd seen the pictures on Instagram.

"Pass the ball, Dean," yelled out Jermaine.

But before the game could restart, Josh grabbed Jermaine's arm and said, "We're not playing like this."

"Israel are cowards," sneered Jermaine, pulling his arm free.

The two boys went forehead to forehead, snarling at each other.

Tamara's red hot chilli temper spurted out like volcanic lava. Racing up to Dean and Lola she cried out, "What are you doing?! The game stops now!"

Her hands were itching to grab those scarves and wrench them down, but she didn't dare. I can't fight both of them, she thought.

Kids were walking away but a few were bunched up on the edge of the area, jeering and letting out piercing whistles. It was impossible to tell which side people were on. Dean and Lola are trying to turn everyone against the Jewish kids, thought Tamara, because of the Israel/Gaza war. And I can't rely on Yaz anymore. Where is she when I need her?

Those left in Josh and Dean's teams were squaring up to each other. Tamara stood with Josh and Hannah. Just behind her, Selma and Gidi had left the chess game and come over.

Tamara was certain a fight would break out and she'd have to protect Gidi.

He's too small for all this, she told herself. Where are the teachers?

Everything had happened so quickly, the duty teacher was patrolling out of sight, round the other side of the building.

She'll turn back soon, Tamara thought, but it might be too late.

Puffing out her chest, trying to look tough, Tamara hoped no one would notice her knees shaking.

Then Lola cried out in a mocking voice, "You're so pathetic, Tamara Cohen. Is-rael."

"Yeah," Dean shot back. "You should stop killing Palestinian babies."

That did it. A deluge of insults about Israel poured out over the area.

"Stop bombing kids!"

"Free Palestine!"

"My dad says Israel should be wiped off the face of the earth."

Tamara turned from one to the other, shocked at how things had turned nasty so quickly. Do they all hate us?

Then Tamara saw Dean take a step to one side, ahead of her, Arthur's ball clutched to his chest. Arthur lunged forward to grab his ball back, but Dean neatly sidestepped again.

Tamara was nearly exploding with fury.

Then Dean yelled out, "Come on, Palestine!"

But instead of dropping the ball and kicking it; in one strange, swift movement, Dean threw the ball hard ahead of himself.

There was a cry and Tamara turned to see Gidi drop to the ground, blood on his face.

It was as if everyone froze and a peculiar silence descended.

Then a voice called out, "What's going on here?"

It was Mr Mackie, Gidi's Maths teacher.

Kids melted away as the teacher bent down and said, "How did this happen, Gidi?"

Tamara turned back to Dean and was about to shout out and accuse the boy.

But in that second, Dean whipped the sunglasses and keffiyeh off his face and she saw a worried frown above his eyes.

She hesitated.

Then Gidi's voice, shaky but clear, rang out, "I fell over playing football, Sir."

Mr Mackie, an uncertain look on his face, looked around at the remainder of the two teams. Dean and Lola had both now removed their scarves and sunglasses. They stood looking unconcerned, arms folded. Jermaine and Josh were standing apart. Zak had disappeared. Arthur looked close to tears, ball clutched to his chest.

The teacher hesitated and then he said, "Come on, let's get you to the First Aider."

Tamara and the teacher helped Gidi up and they all went inside.

Gidi was silent the whole time as they walked to the First Aid room near the school office. He stayed silent as Mrs Broome, the Geography teacher who was also the First Aider, cleaned him up and put some antiseptic cream around his mouth.

Mr Mackie did his best to draw Gidi out but the Israeli boy, with the robotic stare so familiar to Tamara, wouldn't speak.

The bell went for afternoon school, but Tamara didn't move. "I'm not leaving my cousin," she said.

Mrs Broome and Mr Mackie exchanged looks and nodded.

Then Mrs Broome said, "I think Gidi should go home, don't you, Mr Mackie?"

"Yes," said the Maths teacher. "And Tamara should take him. Will your mother be there?"

Tamara nodded. She felt too miserable to speak. She'd completely failed to keep Gidi safe in school. He'd been the subject of horrible racist bullying since his first day and now, less than two weeks later, the bullies had attacked him and hurt him.

What am I going to tell Dad and Mum? she thought as she led the way to their lockers, Gidi shuffling behind her, like on his first day. They'll be furious with me. And they'd be right. It's all my fault. I should never have joined the game. I put Gidi at risk.

My stupid chilli temper. It's messed everything up. Again.

At the lockers, Gidi grabbed his bag, pulled on his jacket and screwed his father's frayed old baseball cap on his head.

As they left school and walked along the street, suddenly Gidi stopped and stood, arms hanging at his side, staring into the distance in full robot mode.

The remains of Tamara's temper, pushed down with all the upset of the day, rushed up through her and in an irritated voice, she said, "Get moving, Gidi, come on. We have to get home. What if Dean and Lola come out of school!"

But Gidi just stood there and Tamara thought she could just start screaming and screaming and screaming. The whole of the past horrible two weeks; the row with Dad; the racist bullying in school; the hatred on the streets against Jews; Yaz going all strange on her about the Israel Gaza war; Dean and Lola setting up the racist football game and, the final straw, Gidi getting hurt.

She couldn't contain it all inside her anymore.

"I did everything wrong!" she burst out.

And as much as the chilli temper was threatening to take over, to Tamara's horror, her eyes filled with tears and a sob escaped from her mouth.

Then she felt a cool hand on her arm and for a second she thought it was Yaz.

But it was Gidi and as she stared into his face, she

saw a kind of transformation.

Gidi's eyes had changed from robotic to round and warm with concern.

Her little cousin was comforting her and calming her down.

"It's OK to feel angry or sad but it's not your fault," Gidi said. "You did nothing on October 7th. The Jews in London did nothing. It happened and everything changed but it's not your fault. That's what Abba says to me when I cry on our video calls . . ."

" . . . I didn't know you cried," cut in Tamara.

"It's embarrassing," said Gidi in a small voice.

They stood in silence for a moment, staring at each other.

Then Gidi said, "I want to go home."

"Let's go," said Tamara.

"No," said Gidi. "I want to go home to Israel."

Gidi started to spill silent tears and Tamara put her arm around his shoulders and led him all the way home, tears pouring down her face.

10

Everyone Takes Sides

When Mum opened the door and saw their tearful faces, she pulled both children inside and wrapped them in her arms without speaking. Tamara could feel Gidi shaking with sobs.

He's missing his mum so much, she thought, which made her cry even more.

Once again, she wondered how she would cope if she had to leave home and go three thousand miles away, with no idea when she could go back.

It's awful, she told herself.

But then she remembered what Gidi had said to her. It's not my fault, she told herself. I can feel sad, but I don't have to feel so guilty all the time.

Her own tears dried up.

Gidi stopped sobbing and drew away, wiping his eyes on the sleeve of his coat.

Mum said, "Kitchen. Hot chocolate and I think

Gidi needs toast and honey."

"Any sausages?" asked Gidi, in a small voice.

Mum and Tamara exchanged grins.

"There's always your favourite kosher beef sausages waiting for you in the fridge," said Mum.

Then they were sitting at the kitchen table, sipping steaming mugs of hot chocolate, sausages sizzling in the frying pan.

Gidi explained that he'd been hurt when the football hit his face at lunch break. "It was a crazy game," he said.

Tamara kept her head bent over her mug.

If that's what Gidi wants to say, she told herself, it's not my business to say anything else.

But she resolved to shadow Gidi every moment he was in school from now on.

"I'm so sorry you got hurt, darling," said Mum in a careful voice. "No one was bullying you or anything? Tamara?"

"No," said Gidi and Tamara at the same time.

"And what about your friends?" said Mum, staring at Tamara. "I presume Yaz came to the rescue."

Tamara kept her eyes fixed on her hot chocolate and muttered, "Yaz was somewhere else, with her cousin."

"Kadija?" Mum said in a sharp voice. Without waiting for a reply, she went on, "I met Amina in the street yesterday – that's Yaz's mum," she said to Gidi, who nodded back. "Amina's worried about how close

Yaz has become with Kadija. They had a sleepover at the weekend."

A pang stabbed straight across Tamara's abdomen.

"Amina's not happy about it," Mum was saying. "Kadija's two years older than Yaz and she and her family have, well, some very strong opinions. Amina asked me if you and Yaz are still friends."

Tamara's eyes welled with tears and she struggled to keep her voice steady. "I'm not sure," she said.

Gidi reached out and put his hand on her arm and the cool palm reminded her so much of Yaz, tears spilled out.

"Oh dear," said Mum. "This seems to be happening everywhere now. People stop talking to each other and so many horrible incidents, because of the Israel/Gaza war. Amina said that her friend's teenage daughter was chased after by men in the street, calling her a terrorist. The girl wears the hijab."

"That's bad," said Gidi. "Racist."

"Yes," said Mum. "Muslims and Jews are both being targeted. You children must be careful in the street."

Mum looked worried and Tamara ducked her head again.

Thank goodness she and Becky had agreed not to talk about the men telling them to get off the pavement. 'This ain't a Jew pavement,' still rang in Tamara's ears.

Then Mum said in a hesitant voice, "There was a message on our Street Neighbours Group." She stopped.

A chill went through Tamara and she said, "Tell us, Mum."

"They saw it on their doorbell cameras and posted the video," went on Mum. "Some man, his face masked, went round the Jewish houses levering mezzuzahs off the door frames."

"That's utterly appalling," cried out Tamara. "Have they gone to the police? If I see that man, I'll . . . I'll . . ."

"Calm down, darling," said Mum. "You mustn't approach anyone like that and remember, your job is to take care of your cousin."

Tamara slumped back in her chair, arms folded, an angry look on her face.

"Of course they went to the police," said Mum. "Dad is thinking of moving our mezzuzah inside because we're worried about Eden and you children."

Tamara opened her mouth to speak but Gidi spoke first.

"I think that's a good idea, Aunty Mel. You can put it back later."

"We'll see," said Mum.

There was silence for a moment and Gidi ate another sausage.

Then Mum said, "We know you're homesick, Gidi, darling. Don't we, Tamara?"

"Yes," said Tamara, nodding, relieved that Mum had changed the subject. "I really do, Gids. You've been so brave since you came here and we really like having you, don't we, Mum?"

"We love it," said Mum. "It's very precious to have this special time with you, Gidi."

Gidi nodded. "*Ken*. It's just that . . ."

He stopped.

"You're homesick," filled in Tamara and Gidi nodded.

"But I'm lucky," he went on. "Asher in my class back home was sent away too. He's miserable. He messaged me. His uncle shouts at him all the time and his big cousins are really mean."

After the snacks, Tamara and Gidi focused on homework and then spent the evening watching Eden's favourite film, all three cousins cuddled up together on the sofa.

Tamara had a restless night and was late getting ready the next morning. By the time they left for school, they had to run the last hundred metres and arrived at the lockers as the bell was sounding. They grabbed their books and went to class.

The first lesson was Geography with Miss Broome. The teacher gave Gidi a warm smile when he entered the room.

Tamara relaxed while Gidi laid out his pencils. Wednesday was her favourite day of the week. PE before lunch and Club after school.

At the end of morning lessons, she waited for Gidi outside the changing rooms and walked with him towards the lunchroom. Josh and Arthur caught up with them.

As they all started chatting about what they wanted to do at Club that evening, Dean and Lola appeared in a group of kids coming out of a classroom up ahead.

Tamara grabbed Gidi's arm, a nervous pang going up through her.

Josh and Arthur bunched around them as Dean said something to Lola and the whole group snickered.

"Get out the way, Is-rael," sneered Lola.

"Jog on!" snapped Tamara but her insides were churning.

She felt Gidi tug her arm and she looked down at his bruised face. His eyes were pleading with her.

"Free Palestine," one of the girls beside Lola called out and she high fived with Dean.

More kids started to pass them in the corridor and some of them joined in, jeering and letting out mocking whistles.

Zak came up and Tamara checked he hadn't decided to put his kippa on. She also checked that her Star of David wasn't on show either.

If any of us show Jewish stuff, she thought, the other kids will go mad. For a tense few moments Tamara and her friends had to walk in the middle of Lola's growing crowd, trying to ignore all the horrible things they were saying.

Then a voice called out, "Clear the corridor, you lot, and get off to lunch."

It was the PE teacher, standing with his hands on

his hips. The jeering stopped abruptly but the teacher didn't comment. Everyone moved off.

As they went into the lunchroom, Tamara thought, People are picking sides and it's only going to get worse. Yaz hasn't even come over to ask me about what happened to Gidi yesterday. And look at the choices: Dean and Lola or me and Gidi. Palestine or Israel.

What if the whole of Y7 splits into two groups, Tamara thought with a shudder, and my group is the smallest? Even with people like Arthur and Selma, who aren't Jewish.

Something bad could happen, like in the football game and I'd have to defend Gidi. As usual, she told herself, the teachers would be looking the other way.

That evening Mum dropped them off at the Spotlight Club. Once in the hall, Tamara and Gidi went over to join Josh, Arthur and Zak.

"That was well bad in school today, everyone calling out stuff about Israel with Dean and Lola," said Arthur.

"People are taking sides. Israel or Palestine," said Tamara. "It's awful."

The others nodded as Selma appeared in a bright green headscarf and waved her chess set at Gidi.

Tamara had already spotted Yaz and Kadija, standing with their friends on the other side of the hall. Selma suddenly said in her direct voice, "Yaz listens to Kadija all the time now."

Tamara shot her a puzzled look. How does Selma know?

As if she guessed Tamara's thoughts, Selma said, "I overheard them in the corridor, saying bad things about Israel. But they never speak against Hamas. My family know that Hamas are militants. I don't understand why Kadija doesn't get it too. And your friend, Yaz."

Gidi gave a snort and Selma rolled her eyes at him. "They think I agree," she went on, "because I'm a Muslim. But my family know that Hamas are terrorists. Dad says Muslims and Jews have so much in common."

"My abba says that too," said Gidi, in an enthusiastic voice.

Gidi gave her a nod and they started to set up the chess game.

Then Jermaine appeared and walked towards Tamara's group.

"Keep over your side," called out Tamara. "You won't want to hang round with Israel kids."

"Yeah," said Josh in a hard voice, fists clenched by his side.

But Jermaine put his hands in his pockets and with his eyes lowered, he walked over and stood next to Zak. He nudged his friend and flicked his head towards Gidi and the others.

"Jermaine wants to say something," said Zak in a

quiet voice. "It wasn't what you think, well, he was angry yesterday . . ."

"*He* was angry!!" cut in Josh. "How do you think we felt?"

"I was upset at all that racism," said Selma, "and I'm not Jewish. My family came here from Syria."

"Oh," said Gidi. "Thought you said Iraq."

"That's my grandmother," said Selma.

"Yes, well, we all come from somewhere," muttered Zak. "I'm Jewish and my family come from Poland. But look, on Sunday evening Jermaine's big brother, Baz, was stopped by the police."

"Why?" said Josh.

"Because he's black," said Jermaine.

"Is he in a gang?" said Selma.

Zak laughed out loud. "You're joking. Baz? He's at college and he wants to be a vet. He's mad about animals and his pets. He's got a cat, a tortoise and three rabbits. The cat had kittens and he has to find homes for them. He's very fussy about who's taking them."

"Mum says if he gets anything else he's moving out," said Jermaine.

Grins broke out around the group.

Then Jermaine said, "Look, Baz was stopped with his friends, who're also black, on their way to the cinema on Sunday night. The police stop black teenagers all the time. They assume they carry knives and stuff. So, I got very angry and Dean and Lola got under my skin. I wanted to hit back at something. That's why I joined in their stupid game. I didn't mean anything. It was wrong."

"Racism against anyone is wrong," said Josh in a grim voice.

"It was very stupid of you to join in with those two muppets," said Arthur. "The war in Gaza's nothing to do with me. My family comes from Thailand. But even I know they were all wrong making people choose sides."

"I know," said Jermaine. "To be honest I don't even get this Israel–Palestine stuff. Why do they shout about it all the time?"

"I don't understand it much either," said Zak.

"It feels like the whole of Year 7 is taking sides," growled Tamara.

"No, it's not that bad," said Gidi in a quiet voice. "Most people didn't join in the football game, did they?"

"Lots of people jeered at us in the corridor today," said Tamara. "The PE teacher heard them and he did nothing. We need to take them on, ourselves." She felt hot as her temper rose and she nodded over at Josh. She knew he was just as angry as she was.

"I'm in," said Josh.

"Well," said Gidi. "Omer and Farrah in my club back in Haifa say we have to find ways to build bridges and make peace when everyone's angry."

"Kadija says, Israelis' don't know how to make peace," said Selma.

Tamara let out a gasp but before she could say anything Gidi's quiet voice cut in.

"That's what a lot of Israelis and Palestinians say," said Gidi. "Peace is pointless. No-one's listening. But me and Yussuf and Omer and Farrah and everyone in Pomegranates for Peace are listening."

How do you make peace with Dean and Lola? Tamara wanted to call out.

But all eyes were on Gidi, so she kept quiet.

"My abba says," went on Gidi, "in Israel there are 160 peace organisations, like Pomegranates for Peace, bringing people together – Israeli Jews and Muslims, kids and adults. After October 7th it wasn't safe to go outside. But me and Yussuf messaged each other all the time and when it was safer we went back to Club."

"I bet you all shouted at each other," said Josh.

"No, we high-fived. We were so happy to be back together with our friends," said Gidi. "Everyone wanted to go back to Club. You have two hours when it doesn't matter, you can speak Hebrew or Arabic, be Muslim or Jewish or nothing."

"I didn't know all that," said Jermaine. "I thought Jews and Arabs just hated each other."

Zak nodded. "Me too. Mum and me don't know anything about peace groups in Israel."

"I didn't know black people were stopped by the police," said Gidi.

Jermaine gave him a nod.

"My dad's Jewish but my mum's Christian," said

Josh. "Mum goes to church but she wants me to learn about both and Dad says we're all in this together."

"Are we?" said Tamara. "Doesn't feel like that."

Loud laughter broke out across the hall.

Looking around Tamara saw Yaz and Kadija were playing table tennis with their group. Yaz looked so happy in her new crowd. It made Tamara feel lonely again.

The others started to move off into their activities.

But Tamara stood there for a few moments longer, watching Yaz.

What did I do wrong? Tamara thought, not for the first time. Why did Yaz turn against me?

And then the questions which kept coming up for Becky and Hannah and so many others flooded in. What did our Jewish friends and family do wrong after October 7th? Why do people turn against Jews here? Gran says we Jews are British citizens, just like them. *We're* not dropping bombs on anyone.

Her head hurt from worrying over all this stuff and there were no answers.

I wish Club was over, she suddenly thought, feeling close to tears. I just want to go home.

11

Emily's Birthday

On Friday night, Gidi helped Tamara set the table for Shabbat.

The whole household had been in a weird state for days. Some of the hostages held in Gaza were going to be exchanged for some Palestinians in Israeli prisons. But no one really knew what might happen and if the deal would fail at the last moment.

Tamara felt like she was living on a tightrope at home, the tension was so bad.

Dad was glued to his phone every evening, scrolling down or speaking to Uncle David, Gidi's dad, on video calls.

Tamara caught snatches when Dad raised his voice sometimes.

" . . . and if they send you into Gaza . . . they might change their minds at the last minute . . . will they let all the children out of the tunnels . . . can't trust anything they say . . ."

Tamara was bursting with questions.

If only Dad would trust me, she thought and tell me *something*. He must know me and Gidi find out stuff online.

Mum wasn't much better. She was always watching the news and then switching over when the children came into the living room.

I can't even talk to Gidi, Tamara told herself now as she put out the cutlery. I don't want to upset him.

But as Gidi took the challah out of its large paper bag from the bakery and placed it on the special board, he said, "Abba says there's a list of hostages and every day they are letting some out."

Tamara stopped and then she said in a careful tone, "I saw it online after school yesterday."

"So did I. Keren messaged me and said they really didn't know until the last minute if anyone would come out," said Gidi. "Yussuf messaged too."

"Oh," Tamara shot him a nervous glance. "What did he say?"

"He said he was glad for both sides."

Tamara thought for a moment and then she said, "Selma said her mum thinks it's a good thing for peace."

The doorbell went. It was Gran. They both went to open the door and Gran drew them in for a big hug. Gidi clung on after Tamara had drawn back, his head buried on Gran's shoulder.

She patted his back. "Everything's going to be fine, darling. You wait and see."

But Tamara didn't feel reassured.

The war had been raging for weeks and even with the release of some hostages, there wasn't any sign of peace. She felt herself begin to spiral down again but Gidi's words earlier this week came back to her. It's not my fault, she told herself and followed Gran and Gidi into the dining room.

Dad was home for Shabbat and came in to take up his place at the top of the table: Mum at the other end, Tamara and Gran on one side and Gidi and Eden opposite.

This is how we sit now on Friday nights, thought Tamara. But I still go up for Dad to bless the children, only Gran puts her hand on my head.

Eden was wriggling about in her seat, excited about something and then she piped up, "It was Emily's birthday this week and Mrs Levy had a cake with candles. Emily's nine."

"No, darling," said Mum shaking her head. "Everyone in your class turns seven this school year. You'll be seven in January . . ."

"The seventh," put in Eden.

"We won't forget your birthday," said Gran, with a smile.

"Yes," said Mum, smiling too. "So, Emily in your class can't be nine."

"Silly Mummy," said Eden giggling. "Emily's not in

my class. And she *is* nine but she can't be home with her family for her birthday, so we did her birthday in class. We all made cards and Mrs Levy's going to post them to her daddy in Israel. My card said 'Happy Birthday Emily. I'm making you a friendship bracelet and we are best friends.' But Sophie had to help me with spelling *friend* because she's top at spellings and . . ."

"She means Emily Hand," said Dad, in a strained voice.

Eden stopped, a bewildered look on her face at Dad's tone.

"Eden doesn't understand," muttered Tamara.

Mum stood up and said, "I'll light the candles."

"Mrs Levy gave us these to light for Shabbat," said Eden, holding out a small packet.

It was the same candles Tamara could see that Mum had brought home before. Everyone was lighting the extra two small candles to remember the hostages.

Eden went to a Jewish school. Mum had been determined when she couldn't persuade Tamara to go to the Jewish high school.

Then Eden said, "I want to light my candles for Emily and Gidi."

"I'm not a hostage in a tunnel," burst out Gidi in an outraged voice. "Don't light for me, I'm not suffering!"

"All right, Gidi," said Dad in a quiet voice.

"Gidi's right," said Tamara, determined to defend her cousin. "What do any of us know about what people are going through?"

She threw Dad a defiant glance. He sat with his shoulders hunched up but to her surprise a confused look crossed his face too.

Then Mum said, "We'll light them for Emily and everyone who isn't home with their families tonight."

Dad's shoulders relaxed and the tense moment passed.

Tamara reminded herself that Dad was still very worried about the family in Israel, especially Gidi's dad, Uncle David.

Please let him keep safe, she thought, as Mum lit the Shabbat candles and said the prayer.

Dad and Gidi said the prayers for the challah and wine and then Dad blessed the children.

But Tamara, standing next to Eden with Gran's warm palm on her head, thought that Dad's voice sounded so tired tonight, as if he'd been beaten down by all the constant horrible news from Israel. She felt her heart go out to her father.

I wish he would talk to me, she thought and tried to send him an encouraging smile. But Dad had sat down and was staring at his plate.

Mum dished up dinner and then Dad began to speak in a quiet voice.

"Emily's father is from Ireland. Did you know that Eden?" he said.

Eden shook her head. She'd cheered up, taken her thumb out of her mouth and was eating her dinner with gusto.

"Well," Dad went on. "Her mum was from Israel, so Emily is an Irish Israeli girl, which is interesting. People in the UK and Ireland talk about her a lot and we are waiting for her to come back home this weekend."

"And she's going to be sooo happy," said Eden in a bright voice. "Because we've sent her a trillion birthday cards."

"That's wonderful, darling," said Mum, but she was frowning towards Dad.

She wants him to stop talking about Emily, thought Tamara. Because we've all agreed not to talk about the situation in Israel and Gaza in front of Eden. She's too young.

But now that Dad had opened the subject, Tamara's head was filling up with a million questions and suddenly she couldn't push them down any longer.

"How do they know Hamas will let Emily go?" she burst out.

Dad's head jerked up but before he could speak, Mum said, "We won't talk about that now, not on Shabbat."

"Quite right," muttered Dad.

But everyone was very subdued for the rest of the meal. Eden hardly finished her dinner and then she put her thumb in her mouth, as she always did when she was worried or upset these days. It was Gidi who saved the day.

"Bead necklaces?" he said, with a grin.

It worked like magic. Eden jumped up, grabbed her cousin's hand and said, "Come on, Gidsy, upstairs."

Dad also pushed back his chair and in a gloomy tone he said, "I need some fresh air."

Tamara saw Gran and Mum exchange looks as Dad went off, pulling the front door shut behind him.

"It's all my fault again," Tamara couldn't help saying, wiping a hand across her eyes. *I'm always close to tears these days.*

But Gran looked outraged. "It is absolutely not your fault, darling," she declared, patting Tamara's hand.

"Of course it isn't," agreed Mum. "Your dad has got himself into such a state. He watches the news all night sometimes. He's obsessed."

"I didn't know that" said Tamara, feeling rather scared. "Perhaps I should stay up with him."

"Of course you can't," said Mum. "You'd never get up for school. But I'm trying to stop him sitting down here, listening to the same news over and over again."

"Poor Dad," said Tamara.

"That's all very well," said Mum. "But it's not doing him or any of us any good. Look at him: he's exhausted, flies of the handle at the least little thing, not even eating properly." Mum pushed her hair back with a tired gesture. "And now you and Yaz aren't friends either, all because of this horrid war."

Tamara stared at Mum's worried face. She hadn't really thought how the tensions of the past few weeks had affected her mother. That's me being selfish again, she told herself.

"Come on," said Gran. "I've bought those chocolate bars you all love as a Shabbat treat." She reached down and opened her bag, pulling our three huge bars, wrapped in gold and silver paper.

"Mum!" cried out Tamara's mother. "That's far too much for the children."

But Tamara laughed out loud with relief and grabbing the bars, set off towards the door. Gidi and Eden will love these, she thought.

In the hallway she hesitated for a moment. Mum and Gran had started to talk about the war again now that she was out of the room. Tamara's ears pricked up to listen.

Gran said, "The Lunch Bunch are going on the march on Sunday."

"Well don't tell Tamara," said Mum. "She's dying to take direct action or whatever. I'm worried she might get into trouble at school. You know what her temper's like."

Tamara felt herself go red and that hot chilli feeling began to rise too.

"I know," said Gran. "We need to keep her calm."

"I'm trying to encourage Tamara to listen to Gidi more these days," said Mum. "He's told me about his club in Israel and how they are working for peace between Israeli Jews and Arabs. I must admit, I didn't know anything about those things."

"I've been to a couple of meetings at our synagogue from one of those peace groups," said Gran. "They speak very well and we had both an Israeli and a Palestinian speaker. I'll let you know next time."

Then both women pushed back their chairs, and Tamara heard the clink of plates as they started to clear the table.

Tamara started to walk down the hallway. I mustn't worry Mum, she told herself. She's got enough worries at the moment.

She remembered something her mother had said after school that day.

"I know things are tense at school these days," Mum had said, as she popped in to see Tamara at her new desk.

"Gidi got hurt," Tamara had suddenly blurted out.

"I guessed as much," said Mum. "But if you don't talk to me, I can't do anything."

"Me and Gidi and our friends are dealing with it."

Mum was quiet for a moment and then she'd said, "All the support you give Gidi, whatever is happening in school – that's working for peace. It's good work, Tamara. Much better than having a fight."

Now as Tamara reached the bedroom door, she thought, My job is to keep my head down at school *and* at home. Until things get better.

Then she went into the bedroom and tossed the chocolate bars on the bed, as Eden screamed out and jumped up and down on her springy toes.

12

Friendship and Kindness

Even though Gidi was kind to Eden over the weekend, spending time with the little girl and making bracelets, it seemed to Tamara that he was in a strange mood.

If Tamara put her head around the door, Gidi would be sitting at the desk, staring at the wall again; his homework books piled neatly on one side and those annoying pencils lined up in perfect order.

Tamara tried to pull him out of it, suggesting they do homework together or go out to meet up with Arthur and the others, but Gidi just shook his head.

He appeared regularly for meals, so Mum didn't notice.

Dad was out most of the weekend, working or meeting a cousin; probably to talk about Israel, Tamara decided. So, he didn't notice anything different either.

"I don't know what to do," Tamara said to Josh in a low voice on a video call, late Saturday afternoon, glancing over her shoulder all the time in case someone came into the bedroom where she did her homework. "It's like he's gone into his own world since Friday night."

Normally she would be having these conversations with Yaz, Tamara thought, as she stared at Josh's face on her screen. It made her feel sad and she had to force herself to concentrate as Josh spoke.

"It's not surprising after that football game and all those nasty things people called out." Josh said.

"There's a lot of nasty stuff around these days," said Tamara. "Yaz's mum told my mum that her eldest had been chased in the street and called a terrorist."

"Yaz didn't tell you, then?" said Josh in a sympathetic tone.

Tamara shook her head. "Both Jews and Muslims have had horrid stuff happen to them since October 7th."

"And Baz because he's black."

They were silent for a moment staring into each other's eyes.

"I'm glad we're friends, anyway," said Josh. "And Arthur too. He never joins in with anything racist."

"Cool," said Tamara.

Then Josh had to go and they ended the call.

But even after talking to her friend, Tamara still didn't know what she should do about Gidi. She was afraid to speak to him about anything; little Emily Hand who'd finally been released with a group of hostages at the weekend; the war in Israel and Gaza, the problems in school. She didn't even feel she could ask him about homework.

He knows I'm here for him, she told herself as they walked to school on Monday morning, but it doesn't feel enough.

As they arrived at school and went to their lockers, Gidi suddenly said, "I'm going to see Mrs Cole."

"OK," said Tamara in a cautious voice. "What about?"

"Everything," said Gidi and then he strode off to class and wouldn't say anything else.

At lunch break, he told her, "I'm going now, will you come with me?"

"Sure," said Tamara.

She wanted to ask a million questions, but Gidi clearly didn't want to speak yet. He was saving it for Mrs Cole.

Keep your mouth shut for once, Tamara Cohen, she told herself, and just be supportive. Gran says that's the way I can work for peace.

Mrs Cole was in her office and beckoned them in.

"What can I do for you both?" She gave them a warm smile.

Tamara looked down and clutched the side of her skirt, feeling suddenly very nervous. What was Gidi planning? She wished she'd asked him before they came in the room.

Gidi started to speak in a low voice. "Kids in our year – not all of them, some of them – aren't good about Israel. They say things which are not true. They say me and the other Jewish kids kill babies. They say Israel should be wiped out. It's not fair and it's upsetting my cousin."

Tamara's mouth fell open and she turned to look at Gidi.

I wasn't expecting that, she thought. But it felt good that her cousin was trying to protect her, instead of the other way round all the time.

Gidi didn't meet her eyes. He was staring at Mrs Cole.

When Tamara looked back at the Head, she thought she saw Mrs Cole's hands shake as she tidied a pile of papers on her desk.

Is Mrs Cole feeling nervous? she wondered.

When the Head spoke, her voice was quite low. "Right, um . . . yes, Gideon, um . . . yes, of course we must do something. Let me . . . um . . . think about it."

Tamara clutched the side of her skirt even more tightly, not trusting herself to speak.

"It's bullying," said Gidi.

"Yes!" burst out Tamara.

The Head remained silent.

Come *on*, Tamara thought. What're you going to *do?*

But Mrs Cole picked up her phone and started to scroll down.

She hasn't a clue, Tamara told herself. Maybe me and Josh should sort it.

Gidi had fallen back into robot mode, arms limp by his side, eyes staring into space.

He's disappointed, Tamara thought with a pang. If the school won't do anything, we've had it.

Then just as Tamara had made up her mind to speak, Mrs Cole looked up.

"I've made a decision," said the Head in a stronger voice. "Last lesson this afternoon, Year 7 will come to the hall for a special assembly."

Tamara gave a shrug. What use is a stupid assembly? she wanted to shout out.

She turned to go without even thanking the Head. But Gidi said, "Yes, Miss. Thank you, Miss."

Like a proper English schoolboy, Tamara couldn't help thinking as they left the office. Normally that would have made her smile, but now all she could think was, What will Dean and Lola do?

"It's better than nothing," said Becky, as they all gathered in the lunchroom.

"Me and Tamara could take Lola out, couldn't we, Tam?" said Josh, leaning over the table, fists clenched.

"No," said Arthur. "Remember what we did with Miss Tate. Don't get angry. Get even."

"How will this stupid assembly stop Lola and her mates whamming into us at every opportunity," snapped Tamara. "I swear, if she touches Gidi . . ."

"She won't," cut in Gidi. "I'd go and tell the Head again."

"You saw how nervous Mrs Cole was," said Tamara. "I don't think she has any idea what to do."

"Let's see what happens this afternoon," said Arthur, in a calm voice.

At the last lesson the teacher met the class in the corridor and took them off to the hall. Tamara and Gidi sat down in a row near the front, with Josh, Arthur, Becky and Hannah. Tamara craned her neck round and saw Yaz sitting in the back row. She didn't catch Tamara's eye. Then to Tamara's annoyance, Lola sat right behind them. At least Dean went further back and sat with some boys from his football squad.

The Head came in and everyone stood up. Mrs Cole took up her place on the platform and said, "Sit down, please."

There was a shuffling as Y7 took their seats.

"It's come to my notice," started Mrs Cole, "that some people are ignoring the way we treat each other at Abbey Park High. Our school motto is, 'Friendship and Kindness at All Times' as you all know. Everyone is welcome in our school, and we won't tolerate bullying. Remember, three strikes and you're out."

She paused and fixed the hall with a firm stare.

That's more like it, thought Tamara.

"Treating everyone with friendship and kindness is

what all the staff expect of you and I'm sure you will agree that friendship is much better for our school than being nasty to each other," went on Mrs Cole.

The Head took a breath and in that second Dean cut in from the back of the Hall, his mocking voice ringing out, "You can't expect me to be kind to Charlie Smith, Miss."

The whole hall burst into shrieks of laughter.

Charlie Smith was a small, nervous boy who seemed to drop things all the time, including a huge bottle of red paint on the Art class floor in his first week in the school. Dean and Lola teased him mercilessly.

"Silence!" called out Mrs Cole.

Dean's form teacher went over and whispered furiously into the boy's ear. Dean just smirked back.

Tamara caught Becky's eye. "This is hopeless," she said in a low voice.

"Right, Is-rael," said Lola behind her, into her ear. "No-one cares about you or your people. Get it?"

She stabbed a finger hard into Tamara's shoulder.

Tamara yelped out.

Mrs Cole fixed her with her eyes and boomed, "That's enough, Year 7."

Lola let out a cackle and then slapped her hand over her mouth in an exaggerated gesture. Tamara slumped down in her chair, arms folded, fuming.

Mrs Cole spent the next ten minutes talking about kindness and friendship until Tamara wanted to scream. She was saved by the home bell ringing out.

Everyone stood up and Mrs Cole had to shout to them to sit down again and wait until she dismissed them.

Tamara felt imprisoned in the middle of a restless, heaving mass of kids, as everyone grumbled and wriggled around her. Angry thoughts washed about inside her as she sat, legs stuck out, arms folded.

Finally, they could leave and everyone streamed out of the hall.

As they walked to the lockers, Tamara cried out, "That was pointless!"

"Yeah," snarled Josh. "Utter waste of time."

Josh slammed his locker door shut and walked off in a fury. Arthur ran to catch him up. "I feel just the same," said Tamara to Gidi.

Gidi shrugged. His face was very pale and Tamara's heart went out to him.

I don't want to upset him anymore and make things worse, she told herself and they walked home in silence.

Next morning, when they arrived in school, to Tamara's horror there was a swastika drawn on her locker door in black felt pen. Gidi tried to wipe it off with his shirt sleeve, but it had dried. "It might be permanent ink," he said.

Tamara kicked the lockers in a terrible temper and one of the teachers, a young man who'd just started at the school, yelled, "Oi. Pack that in."

"Why should I?" Tamara yelled back. "Look at my locker . . . Sir."

The teacher came over and stared at the swastika. "Go and tell the caretaker, he'll have something to remove that." Then he walked off, hands in his pockets.

"Is that it?" Tamara called after him. "Nothing to say, Sir?"

But the teacher didn't turn round or give her any sign he was bothered.

One of the caretakers came past.

"Please, Sir, can you clean this off?" she said.

The man had grey hair and was much older than Dad, Tamara thought.

Frowning at the locker door, he said, "That ain't right. Me dad fought in the war to get rid of them Nazis. Hope they ain't back. I'll clean it off, sweetheart. Be good as new. You'll see."

But despite the kindness of the old caretaker, who had cleaned away the swastika before the end of morning lessons, Tamara couldn't help feeling a sense of defeat.

Gidi was so brave going to the Head, she told herself. But what did he get out of it?

Dean and Lola and quite a few others had started to call out horrible things to her in the corridors, as if the assembly had given them permission. Tamara felt haunted and powerless to retaliate, in case the Head accused her of not being kind to people.

"Am I being kind enough, Is-rael?"

"Who'd wanna be friends with you?"

"Is this kind enough for you?" That was Lola who pushed Tamara from behind more than once.

Tamara found herself looking over her shoulder all the time, her head swivelling whenever she heard whispers. She felt more and more lonely and targeted as the week wore on, even though she kept close to Gidi. Josh was hanging with Zak and she often saw them looking quite angry as if they were plotting something. But she didn't join in because it would upset Gidi. Arthur played football at every possible moment, as his team had a big match coming up. Selma had decided it was her job now to keep Tamara updated about Yaz and told her that she'd overheard Kadija saying Yaz was off school with a bad cold and wouldn't be back before the weekend.

Tamara didn't know whether to feel relieved or concerned.

Should I video call her? she wondered for ages. In the end she decided to send a message.

sorry ur sick get better soon x

Her heart was beating as she pressed Send. What if Yaz ignores me or sends back something or horrible, or shows it to Kadija and they laugh at me?

But a few seconds later her phone pinged.

thanx tam see u next week xx

Tamara felt her heart soar and for a moment she thought, We're back!

Then her mood plunged back down. What did Yaz's message really mean? She didn't say let's meet up at the weekend.

Yaz is bound to feel better by then, Tamara told herself. Colds don't last that long.

But she kept the message on her phone and looked at it from time to time for comfort.

Meanwhile, the news of the war was getting worse. So many people were dying in Gaza, children just like her and Gidi, and no more hostages were being released. The terrorists even had a tiny baby hidden away in those horrible tunnels.

"How could they take a baby hostage?" Mum said one morning in an anguished voice, when Eden was upstairs brushing her teeth.

Tamara felt angry and upset all the time. She could hardly concentrate on her homework. Sitting in the evenings in Mum and Dad's room, she found herself staring blankly at the wall. She completely forgot to do the Science homework and got a demerit on Friday and her handwriting was so bad for the History homework she was told to do it again or she'd also get another demerit.

Gidi was no better. He seemed to have shrunk into permanent robot mode and they walked to and from school in silence most days.

Mum tried to cheer them up in the evenings. "It's Chanukah next week. You should invite some of your friends over for donuts and latkes," she said at dinner on Thursday night.

Gidi looked down at his plate.

Tamara shrugged and said nothing.

Even little Eden only murmured, "I don't care about dreidels."

Tamara loved playing the dreidel game every year. The dreidel was a kind of spinning top, and she especially liked ones that lit up or played a tune. Eden had only mastered spinning the dreidel last year and found it very exciting.

They played for sweets. When the dreidel stopped, depending on how it fell, you might have to give the other person a sweet, double sweets, have another go or nothing. Each year they made up new rules and Tamara had been looking forward to playing the dreidel game with Gidi. Yaz always came round too and she loved Chanukah just as much as Tamara.

But this year there would be no Yaz, Tamara told herself.

It felt as if there was nothing to look forward to. Not even Mum's famous potato latkes – little cakes made from grated potatoes and onion and deep fried. They were the most delicious crispy snack in the world, but Tamara could only taste defeat in her mouth.

There's nothing we can do about the racism at school, she told herself. The teachers don't care and the Head simply doesn't know what to do.

Her whole friendship group had changed in the

past couple of weeks too. Tamara was grateful that Becky and Hannah had drawn closer and Selma and Gidi were becoming good friends too. But there was no one in her life like Yaz.

Yaz understands me better than anyone, Tamara told herself. At least, she used to, before she went off with Kadija.

So now most of my friends are Jewish, she realised. If Jewish kids are going to hang out with mainly Jewish kids at school, maybe I should have gone to the Jewish high school after all, was her last thought before she fell asleep on Friday night.

13

Keren

After a restless night, Tamara woke up on Saturday morning later than usual. Eden's bed was empty and the house seemed strangely silent.

She pulled on leggings and a long-sleeved T-shirt and went down to the kitchen.

Everyone was sitting in silence.

Gidi and Eden look as miserable as me, she told herself, slumping down into a chair.

Dad was settled at the table and seemed quite happy for once, as he tucked into a huge plate of fried eggs, kosher beef sausages, baked beans and hash browns.

Must have had some good news from Uncle David in Israel, Tamara told herself. Can't think what.

"How many hash browns, darling?" said Mum in a cheery voice.

Tamara looked over at Gidi's plate. It had a single sausage on it and he was pushing it around instead of wolfing it down as usual.

Eden had her favourite doll on her lap and was plaiting the doll's hair instead of eating.

Tamara felt her stomach close up. "Just a cup of tea, Mum," she said in a tired voice.

Dad looked up with a frown on his face.

Tamara ducked her head.

What have I done now? she thought.

But then Dad started talking in a cheery tone like Mum, his eyes crinkling as if he was about to tell a good joke. "I've got a surprise for everyone."

Even Eden didn't look up, Tamara noted.

Gidi let out a sigh.

"You're all so miserable," said Dad, in a voice that suggested everyone should laugh.

"It's been a long autumn term," Mum said, signalling to Dad with both eyebrows raised.

Dad didn't seem to notice. "Well, don't you want to know what the surprise is?" he said, looking round the table.

Gidi slowly shook his head and Eden stuck her thumb in her mouth.

"Not really," said Tamara. "There are surprises every day and they're all horrible."

Dad leaned back in his chair and said, "Keren arrives tomorrow afternoon."

It was as though a volcano had erupted under the kitchen floor.

All three children pushed back their chairs –

Tamara's fell over with a crash – leapt to their feet and screamed out, "Yesss!!"

Then they all started talking at once.

"What time's she arriving?"

"What shall I wear?"

"We can make friendship bracelets."

"I can ask Keren about Yussuf. She must have seen him," said Gidi.

"She'll have to sleep on the couch downstairs I suppose." This was Mum.

"No!" said Gidi, in such a big voice, everyone stopped and stared at him.

"Keren and Tamara will sleep together in Tamara's room," went on Gidi. "I will sleep on the sofa."

"But, Gidi, darling . . ." Mum began.

"No, Aunty Mel," Gidi cut in, with a firm shake of his head. "Tamara has been the best cousin in the world giving up her bedroom for me and I know it hasn't been easy."

"But she loves sharing with me, don't you, Tamsy Wamsy?" wailed Eden around her thumb. She was on the verge of tears.

Tamara rushed around the table, pulled Eden onto her lap and said, "I LOVE sharing a room with you, darling Eden. Don't worry, Gidi. We'll manage."

"I've decided," said Gidi. "And I won't change my mind. Please can I have my proper breakfast now, Aunty Mel? I'm starving."

And that was that.

Gidi ate such a huge breakfast, even Dad commented. Eden and Tamara shared hash browns and sausages and planned all the things they would do with Keren.

Mum said they would borrow a sleeping bag for Gidi and then rushed upstairs to strip his bed and wash his sheets so that they'd be dry for Keren the next day.

As Tamara settled down to homework after breakfast, determined to finish everything and then get her bedroom ready for her amazingly cool fifteen-year-old cousin arriving, she felt happier than she'd been all week.

This is going to be great, she told herself as she fired up her laptop.

Saturday and then Sunday morning flew by with all the preparations.

Eden made a pile of bracelets and necklaces.

Gidi moved his school stuff to the desk in Mum and Dad's room.

Tamara moved back into her own room. She would still sleep on the chair bed but it was a bigger room than Eden's so at least she didn't have to sleep with her nose jammed against the wall.

Mum baked and shopped and then baked some more.

Dad took the car out to fill it up with petrol and spent a lot of time on his laptop, video chatting with everyone in Israel. He left for the airport before lunch on Sunday and then there was nothing to do except wait.

And wait.

And wait.

"I'll go mad if they don't get here soon," moaned Tamara as the hours ticked by.

"Abba says the flights from Israel are very unreliable," said Gidi, looking anxious. "Maybe Keren hasn't even left yet."

"Why doesn't Dad give us an update?" said Tamara.

Gidi shrugged.

Tamara decided to go up to her bedroom and see what clothes she could share with Keren. Some of my tops will fit her, she told herself, as she raced upstairs. But as she reached her room, there was the sound of Dad's car pulling onto the drive.

"They're here," she cried out and heard Eden squealing below.

Leaping the stairs two at a time, she rushed outside through the front door, already wrenched open by Gidi, as Keren stepped out of the car, her face quite pale.

"That was a humungous trip," she said in a tired voice.

Gidi rushed up and threw himself into his big sister's arms. They stood on the drive, Keren's eyes closed as her head rested on her little brother's shoulder.

Tamara felt close to tears.

They've missed each other so much, she thought.

And then she just had to pull Eden in for a cuddle. What if we were suddenly separated by some awful event? Tamara thought with a stab of fear. I couldn't bear it.

But Eden wriggled free and cried out, "We waited and waited and now you're here and we can all play together, can't we, Gidsy Widsy?"

That made everyone laugh.

Gidi and Keren pulled apart and Gidi insisted carrying Keren's huge case into the house. He had to lift it with both hands and it still dragged on the path.

"What on earth have you brought, darling?" asked Mum with a grin, gathering the girl into her arms for a hug.

"Surprises," said Keren and, catching Tamara's eye, she gave her a long, slow wink.

Tamara felt a thrill go through her.

Mum insisted on Keren coming into the kitchen for sandwiches and "a nice cup of tea, after such a long journey," she told her niece.

"I don't drink tea, Aunty Mel," said Keren, checking the filling on a sandwich. "Do you have any cola?"

Gid took a can out of the fridge, pulled the tab and handed it to his sister with a flourish.

"Isn't anyone else eating?" asked Keren, grinning at her brother.

Tamara and Eden were still full from lunch, but Gidi polished off most of the sandwiches.

"I don't eat as much as my brother, you'll be relieved to hear," said Keren.

"Well," said Mum. "You need a proper cooked meal tonight. I'm making spaghetti bolognese."

"Great," said Keren. Then she fixed her eyes on the others and said, "Shall we open my suitcase upstairs?" Eden leaped to her feet with a squeal and she and Gidi raced off.

Tamara suppressed a desire to run after them. Too immature, she told herself.

"You go first," she said and felt quite grown-up following her tall, slender cousin up to the bedroom.

Keren took after her mother. They were both tall, with long, fair hair and dark eyes and eyebrows. Uncle David and Tamara's father were square shaped, with broad shoulders and dark hair which they kept very short. Like Gidi's hair, thought Tamara as they reached her bedroom.

"We're sharing," said Keren. "So is Gidi in with Eden?"

Eden let out a shriek and said, "I'm not sharing with a *boy! Uugh.*" She put her fingers to her nose and squeezed it as if there was a bad smell in the room.

Gidi laughed and said, "I'm on the sofa in a sleeping bag. Like camping."

Keren smiled and that was the end of it, to Tamara's relief.

Dad had already brought the heavy suitcase upstairs and put it on the bed. Keren unzipped the case as Eden plopped down onto the pillows, Gidi sat on the chair bed and Tamara sat cross-legged on the end of her bed.

The room felt cosy and full all at the same time and Tamara realised how much she had missed being in her own space.

How can I ever move back with Eden when Keren goes? she wondered. But for now, she decided to enjoy every minute.

Keren threw back the lid of the suitcase and pulled out a large supermarket bag with Hebrew letters on the side. She dropped it into Eden's lap. Eden pulled the bag open and reached inside. Out came bags and bags of brightly coloured beads and rolls of multicoloured string for necklaces and bracelets. Screaming as each bag tumbled onto the duvet, the little girl cried out, "I love them. They're . . . they're . . ."

" . . . awesome," filled in Tamara.

Gidi groaned. "Thanks, Sis. I'm going to be sooo busy from now on."

They all laughed and then Eden started to make a bead necklace.

Meanwhile Keren had been pulling aside jeans and long sleeve t-shirts, muttering, "Not this, not this, here we are!"

She pulled out a heap of clothes and handed them to Tamara. "Just a few bits. Nava put some stuff in too. Thought you might like some Israeli fashions."

Tamara was overwhelmed as she held up top after top, two gorgeous pairs of sparkling leggings, unlike anything in the shops in London and some really cool skirts. She couldn't wait to try them on.

"Hope there's a party somewhere," said Keren with a grin.

Tamara felt her eyes widen as an anxious stab went up through her. "Um, well, I'll ask around."

She suddenly felt a fool. Who was going to have a party unless it was their birthday? All her friends' birthdays were over.

"Only kidding you," said Keren and then she closed the case.

She looked over at Gidi, who was staring at the floor.

"Hey, little brother, you didn't want a sparkly top too, did you?"

Tamara looked over at her cousin, feeling guilty. I've been enjoying myself so much I haven't given him a thought.

Gidi shook his head and then he said something in Hebrew.

Keren shot him a teasing grin. "Oh, you thought Dad would send you something over. Hmm."

Then she lifted her jumper to show a small bag with several zips, secured around her waist. She pulled open one of the zips, took out an envelope and handed it to Gidi.

"Dad sent you this."

Gidi opened the packet and a wad of English notes fell out.

Tamara gasped and Eden cried out, "It's thousands

and thousands – you can buy a car."

They all laughed except Gidi, who began counting the five-pound, ten-pound, and twenty-pound notes.

"One hundred pounds," said Gidi when he'd finished and then, frowning, he said, "How did Dad get English money?"

"They always keep English money in the house, for when we come to London," said Keren.

"But . . . but . . . Dad needs the money, for Mum and the hospital and . . ."

"Sheket! Quiet, little brother. You need pocket money or new trainers or stuff, I don't know," said Keren, grinning. She shook her head at Tamara. "He's always like this, worrying about everyone except himself. Stop feeling so guilty, habibi."

Gidi's face cleared and he grinned, stashing the money away in the pocket of his jeans. Then Keren pulled a book out of her bag and handed it to Gidi. "From Yussuf. Said he's missing you," she said.

Gidi took the book and another grin lit up his face. "It's Yussuf's favourite chess book. We use it every week when we play in Club." He flicked through it. "Awesome, he's marked the moves he wants me to learn. I'm going to video call him right now."

He leapt off the bed, grabbed his phone and went downstairs.

"Result?" said Keren with a grin.

"Yep, cool," said Tamara, shooting back a shy smile at her older cousin.

* * *

The rest of the day flew by and then Tamara was under her duvet on the chair bed, Keren settled too, and just as she'd planned, they kept each other awake, talking about clothes and body influencers and music and make up. Keren said she'd split up with her boyfriend and was missing him and she asked Tamara if *she* had a boyfriend which made Tamara laugh.

They fell silent for a few moments and then Keren said in a more serious voice, "Gidi told me about some anti-Israel stuff in your school."

Tamara felt herself go hot. "Um . . . well . . . yes," she said. "Some kids at school have been horrible."

"Those bruises around his mouth. What happened, Tam?"

Tamara had been dreading this question. She almost threw her duvet off, as she felt herself become hotter and hotter. In a wobbly voice, Tamara said, "Hit in the face with a football, and I'm so so sorry, Keren, I really am. He's your little brother."

"Hey!" said Keren in a soothing voice. "It wasn't your fault."

"I should have done more to protect him from the bullies," blurted out Tamara. "Dean and Lola and their crowd. They influence other kids, who honestly have no idea about Irael and Palestine, or even where they are on a map. So, things got a bit out of hand . . ." Tamara tailed off.

"What did the school do?" asked Kerren.

"Not much," said Tamara and Keren gave a sarcastic snort.

"But Gidi's so brave," Tamara said. "And he's, well, so sensible, he doesn't get into fights. He tries to sort things out. Not like me. Always shooting off my mouth and getting into trouble."

Keren gave a low laugh. "He told me about your chilli temper."

"Gidi doesn't lose his temper, he talks about peace all the time," said Tamara.

"Yep. That's my Gidi. Honestly, I think he should be a Peace Ambassador in the UN," said Keren.

That made them giggle and Tamara felt herself calm down.

It was as though she could say anything into the dark room.

"What's on your mind, Cuz?" Keren said.

"Well," started Tamara, "it's just that, you know Gidi has those pencils you gave him."

"Yes, I remember," said Keren.

"Well, he . . . he . . . has this thing he does, it's a bit weird."

There was silence. Tamara wondered if Keren had fallen asleep.

But Keren said, "Go on."

"In class," Tamara went on, "he gets all his pencils out, lines them up in exactly the same way every single time and then folds his arms and stares into space, like a robot."

There was another silence, deeper than the previous one.

Then Keren gave a snuffle and said, "He started doing that in the bomb shelter. We have to go down six floors to the basement, and you can't use the lift. Too dangerous in an air raid. The electricity could go off and you'd get trapped. Gidi was so scared – well, we all were."

"It must have been awful," said Tamara.

"It wasn't just on October 7th, the sirens have been going off every day since and in the middle of the night. Mum hasn't been well for a while. She's in and out of hospital. Women's stuff, she says, when I ask. She has a good friend who looks after her when Dad is away."

Keren stopped and Tamara lay very quiet in her bed, not daring to speak.

"Dad wasn't with us most of the time, either. He was at the hospital in Haifa and now he's at an army hospital in the south." Her voice broke a little.

Tamara reached out and felt for her cousin's arm and patted it a little.

Keren gave a sniff and went on, "So I had to look after Gidi most of the time. I didn't know what to do, he couldn't cope with the air raids and I was worried about his mind, his . . ."

She was trying to find the right words in English, Tamara realised.

"His mental health?" she said.

"Yes," said Keren. "Gidi doesn't understand much about Mum's health either but he worries a lot. I don't think he understands much about why Mum is in hospital. I wanted to take his mind off the sirens and the air raids. Yussuf's mum was very kind to us in the shelter, so that helped."

Keren's voice was lower now and Tamara had to strain to hear all the words.

"After a few days," went on Keren, "I found a pack of new pencils at the back of my drawer. I put them in a pencil case and gave them to Gidi in the bomb shelter with a pad of paper and told him to draw something. That's when he started to line them up in that special way and stare at them. He did that every single time. I was so worried, I spoke to Yussuf's mum about it. She said it's called something, I forget, but it's when you do the same thing all the time to feel safe. It's caused by trauma. Gidi was traumatised on October 7th and it's only the pencils that kept him calm."

They were silent for a bit and then Tamara said, "I told him to wait until everyone sits down and then get the pencils out. No one notices by then. The Geography teacher tells him he's very organised."

"That's awesome! What a great idea, Tam, and it's good if he's praised. Yussuf's mum said to do lots of praise."

"Oh well, that's easy then," said Tamara, beaming in the dark because Keren thought she'd done well.

"Let's just praise him all the time."

"Only not when he eats everything on the table," said Keren, giggling.

That set Tamara off and Mum put her head round the door.

"Too noisy, girls, it's late and you both have school in the morning."

"Both?" said Tamara.

"Yes, we thought it would be nice if Keren came with you. Dad spoke to the school last week when he knew Keren was coming over."

Tamara settled down under her duvet.

Everything's so much better now Keren's here, she told herself as she drifted off.

14

Taking the Lead

Keren came down to breakfast on Monday morning wearing skinny black jeans, a black sweater and a short wool jacket. She looked so cool. Tamara felt like a baby in her uniform.

"Will this be OK for school, Aunty Mel?" asked Keren.

"That's fine, darling," said Mum, nodding with approval. "Gidi, here's some extra dinner money. Make sure Keren eats lunch."

"Keren eats nothing," said Gidi with a grin and put the money in his pocket.

Then it was time to leave and Tamara handed Keren a thick wool scarf which she wound round and round her neck until only her face and part of her hair was showing.

It was a crisp sunny morning with a deep blue sky. All the skiddy piles of wet autumn leaves had disappeared, and the pavements were clear and dry as they all walked off.

"It's December 4th today," said Keren. "Chanukah starts on Thursday night. What do you do?"

"Usual stuff," said Tamara. "Presents, donuts, latkes. Eden wants us all to make endless paper chains to decorate the living room. Just warning you."

Gidi groaned. "Not me. I made all the friendship bracelets."

"Pini and I met on Chanukah last year," said Keren in a wistful voice. Pini was the boyfriend she'd split up with in Israel.

"You could send him a nice GIF, wish him Happy Chanukah," said Tamara in a cautious voice.

Keren brightened up. "Good idea, Tam. You can help me choose the GIF."

"Sure. But not in school. If the teachers see us with a phone, they confiscate it forever."

Keren laughed and then they arrived at the school gates and went to the lockers.

Morning lessons went well, and Keren even put her hand up. Everyone was curious to see the older teenager in their classes, not wearing uniform, but no one said anything weird, to Tamara's relief.

"Who cuts your hair?" asked Becky at the end of morning school as they walked towards the lunchroom.

"My friend's sister. She does hairdressing at college," said Keren as if it was the most natural thing in the world.

"Lucky you," said Becky. "I bet she knows all the latest fashions."

Tamara was walking ahead of them when Yaz appeared. There was no sign of Kadija. Tamara stopped, not sure what to do.

Yaz gave her a small smile and said, "Hi, Tam."

"On your own?" said Tamara.

"Kadija caught my cold, she's off school," said Yaz.

"OK. You feeling better?"

Yaz nodded.

Tamara glanced round. The others were bunched up in a group chatting to Arthur and Josh. For a moment a warm feeling flooded her. It felt like old times, hanging with Yaz, talking about stuff.

"Haven't seen Keren for ages," said Yaz, nodding towards the group.

"It was a surprise for Gidi. She only arrived yesterday," said Tamara. "She's staying for Chanukah."

Yaz's eyes lit up and she said, "Mum said it must be Chanukah soon. She loves your mum's potato latkes."

In a rush of warmth, Tamara said, "Come over one day. Like you always do."

There was a pause as the two old friends stared at each other.

Tamara could see her own confusion reflected in Yaz's eyes. Then she blurted out, "Don't bring Kadija."

Yaz stiffened and said in a hurt tone, "Kadija's my cousin."

"Oh yes." Tamara didn't want to be disrespectful to Yaz's family.

But then in a sudden rush, she plucked up the courage to say something which had been on her mind ever since Yaz went off with Kadija. "I haven't changed, Yaz. I'm the same person, whatever you and your cousin think. I can't help it that Israel and Gaza are at war. It's not my fault."

Yaz stood there for a moment, staring at Tamara, still with that confused look on her face. Then she shrugged and said, "OK."

She walked off away from Tamara, past Keren and the others, her head down, bag swinging on her shoulder. She's like a stranger, thought Tamara. As if all our friendship just dissolved away like sugar in coffee. Kadija has her now. All because of this stupid war. Me and Yaz are over.

Keren came up with Gidi, Becky and the others and they all walked towards the lunchroom. No one noticed that Tamara had gone very quiet. Becky and Keren were deep in conversation about Israeli fashions.

Suddenly a voice up ahead snarled, "Out of my way."

It was Lola, striding towards them, elbowing a girl to the side.

Oh no, what now? thought Tamara.

Lola came to halt and a couple of girls in her crowd bunched round her.

Tamara squared up to them and blocked their way to her cousins. "You get out of our way," she snapped.

"Awesome, Is-rael!" said Lola in a mocking voice. "So now you brought half your flipping country with you." She raised her hand, palm out as if to push Tamara.

But Keren had moved round her cousin and loomed over Lola who was three years younger and shorter, despite her broad frame.

Lola was so surprised she took a step backwards.

"I can speak with you, English girl," said Keren in a cool voice. "About politics. But first you maybe have to find politics in your English dictionary. I can help you."

One of the mean girls let out a giggle and Lola went brick red.

"Get out of my way, Israel," growled Lola.

Keren took some steps forward, and Lola's group instinctively made way for the older girl.

"Sure. *Yoffee Toffee*," said Keren with a grin.

Some boys in their class went past calling back, "*Yoffee Toffee*. Hey, Gidi."

Gidi raised a hand to them, and they all laughed.

"This ain't over, Is-rael," growled Lola, as she and her group moved on.

"Anytime, English girl," called back Keren in a cheery voice.

"Awesome," said Gidi. "I wish you came to this school. She's been horrible since my first day."

"She's not a nice girl," said Keren, flicking her long hair over her shoulder.

"She needs a slap," growled Tamara and strode off into the lunchroom.

Once they were seated with their food trays, Keren said to Gidi, "Is she the one who hurt your face?"

"No," said Tamara, "that was Dean. Over there." She nodded to a table further away.

Keren craned her neck to see and then looked back. "We don't get this racism in Israel," she said. "We just have the war."

That made them all very quiet for a few moments.

Then Keren said to Gidi, "What happened on your video call last night with Omer and Farrah?"

Gidi brightened up. "It was great. Yusuf was there too. He's going to message me with a new chess move."

"OK," said Keren. "Were you going to ask them something else?"

Gidi stared across the table and Tamara saw that robotic look shadow his face. He's worried about something, she thought and a pang crossed her tummy.

"I asked them if they can speak to our school," said Gidi, in a shaky voice.

Tamara frowned. "Why?"

"Omer and Farrah can speak about peace, better than me. But I decided it was a bad idea. Dean and Lola would shout stuff out and people would join in," said Gidi.

Tamara exchanged looks with Keren and the older girl gave Tamara an anxious shake of her head.

"Lola's been a nightmare ever since that stupid

friendship assembly last week," growled Josh, clenching his fists. "People like her and Dean, they're so racist. It's time we did something ourselves. Are you in, Tam?"

Tamara was lost in thought, as she looked round at her cousins and her friends. But then her eyes rested on Gidi's face, so spaced out, like when he first arrived. She thought she would never shake him out of it. He's come such a long way, she realised. He's made friends and everyone calls out *Yoffee Toffee* now. I can't let him go backwards. I have to do something. It's my job, like Mum said. My way of working for peace.

And then, suddenly, she could see the way forward.

"No, Josh," Tamara said in a firm voice. "I'm not in. Not this time. I think Gidi has done something amazing again."

Gidi's head jerked up and she saw a flicker of hope in his eyes.

"What?" said Josh.

"He's found a way to do something for peace, even when everything feels hopeless, here in school and over in Israel and Gaza."

Keren said in a rush, "You can't imagine how terrible it is in Israel. Kids can't sleep and they wet the bed because they're scared terrorists are going to break in and kidnap them. And in Gaza the children are terrified because of the bombing."

There was a pause and then Tamara said, "Just because there's a war now, it's not a reason to give up on peace. That's what you would say, Gidi, isn't it?"

Gidi nodded, his eyes fixed on his cousin and then he said in a small voice, "And Omer and Farrah."

"You can't change people like Lola," said Josh, a grim look on his face.

"But you can change some people," said Tamara.

"Well said, Cousin," said Keren with an approving nod. "If anyone knows how to bring people together, it's Omer and Farah."

"I can't imagine Lola and Dean and their mean friends listening to anyone from Israel," said Josh.

"But other people will listen," said Gidi.

Tamara stared over at her cousin and her heart rose as she saw a new light in his eyes. "Go on, Gidi," she said.

"Those kids who joined in shouting stuff in the football game," went on Gidi in a firmer voice. "They don't know anything about Israel or Palestine. It was just fun for them. I think some of them would listen to Omer and Farrah."

"That's how all the peace groups start out in Israel," said Keren.

"What? There's more than one?" said Arthur.

"Many groups," said Keren. "When they started there were problems. Israeli Jews and Muslims wouldn't go. Some parents refused to let their kids join the clubs. But then people gave it a try and the kids loved it. The grown-ups meet up too and make friends."

"Abba says there are 160 grassroots peace organisations in Israel now," said Gidi. "And they've all kept going even after October 7th."

"There's many different groups," put in Keren. "Like the Freddy Krivine tennis camps . . ."

"What's tennis got to do with peace?" said Arthur with a grin.

"The Jewish and Arab kids play tennis together and they find out they can all have fun and make friends. It's a great idea," said Keren.

"What else?" asked Becky.

"Lots," said Keren. "Stand Together, Kids4Peace, Hand in Hand, The Parents' Circle and they're all like Gidi's club, Pomegranates for Peace."

"You never see it on the news," said Arthur.

"Exactly," said Tamara and pushing her chair back, she stood up. "That's why we have to do something. I'm going to the Head to make her . . ." She paused and took a breath. "No, I didn't mean that. I'm going to ask the Head politely that she invites Omer and Farrah onto a video call for assembly this week. Peace can't wait any longer. Keren and Gidi, you coming?"

The two siblings exchanged looks and then they both jumped up at the same time.

"Awesome, Cousin," said Gidi.

His eyes were so bright Tamara felt dazzled for a moment.

Result! she thought.

The three cousins dumped their lunch trays on the trolley near the door and walked off to the Head's office. When they reached the door, Tamara felt butterflies in her tummy and gave Keren an anxious look. Keren gave her an encouraging smile. Tamara nodded back and knocked on the office door.

"Come in," came the Head's voice.

Tamara opened the door, and they all walked in.

"Hello, everyone," said Mrs Cole with a warm smile. She looked at Keren. "You must be Gideon's sister, Karen, isn't it?"

"It's Keren, Mrs Head Teacher," said Keren and everyone grinned.

"Ah, yes," said Mrs Cole. "Keren. A lovely name. Welcome to Abbey Park High School. I hope everyone is looking after you."

Keren shrugged and then she said, "Not everyone."

Mrs Cole frowned. "Tamara. What's happened?"

Tamara was clutching the side of her skirt, her insides churning. It felt like one of those really big moments in her life and she had to get it right.

Taking a breath, she said, "No, everything isn't OK. There are bad things said by some kids in our year. Keren's heard it now."

Mrs Cole looked puzzled. "I thought I'd dealt with all that in assembly last week."

Tamara stared at the Head for a moment and all she could think was. This is hopeless.

But her cousins were looking at her and Tamara felt her chilli temper rise as she thought of Gidi slipping backwards.

I have to do this, she told herself.

"It needs more than talking about friendship, Miss," she said in a wobbly voice. "I'm sorry. But it does."

Mrs Cole's eyebrows shot up, but she didn't interrupt.

"I think that Gidi's club leaders, Omer and Farrah, should speak to everyone in our year. They know how to get people to think about peace and getting together and . . ."

" . . . building bridges across divided communities," put in Keren in quite a grownup voice.

Mrs Cole looked impressed and she said, "Do they live in London?"

"No, Miss," said Tamara. "In Israel."

"Well, if they come over," said Mrs Cole, "I can invite them to speak in assembly. Though I'm not sure I quite understand what they can do."

"They can't come here," said Tamara. "But we could ask them to speak on video, like when there was that assembly on climate change and the Professor in America came on the big screen in the hall and spoke to the whole of Y7."

Tamara stopped, her mind racing. Am I crazy? What if no one listens?

But Mrs Cole was nodding in a thoughtful way. "Hmm," she said. "Tell me more about Omer and Farrah and your club."

So Keren explained about Pomegranates for Peace and how Jewish and Muslim Israeli kids went to the club together. Gidi put in about his friend Yussuf.

Then he said, "Omer and Farrah say, everyone in Israel – Jew, Muslim, Bedouin, Druze, Christian, everyone – should feel they're equal and working towards a better society as Israeli citizens."

"I didn't know there were so many different communities in Israel," said Mrs Cole. "I thought it was just Jews and Arabs. You're teaching me a lot about your country, Gideon."

"We have to find ways to build a bridge for peace," said Keren. "Or there will always be horrible wars. Gidi and me have to join the army in a few years."

Tamara shuddered at the thought of her cousins fighting in a war. What if they were killed? It spurred her on to speak again.

"I . . . We . . ." Tamara looked at the others and they nodded. "We think that people in school don't know anything about Israeli Muslims and Jews. Or Palestinians. They can't even find the countries on a map. They've heard slogans and they yell them out without thinking. They have no idea about peace groups. If the kids in our school heard Omer and Farrah speak, it might make things a bit better. Anyway, nothing else is working right now."

Mrs Cole stared at her and Tamara thought, I shouldn't have said the last bit.

But the Head said in a thoughtful voice, "You've all spoken very well. I have been concerned about the atmosphere in school."

Tamara was so relieved she let go of her skirt.

"I'm pleased to see you taking the lead, Tamara," the Head went on with an approving nod. "That hot temper of yours has a use, you know. Instead of losing control, harness that powerful energy to take a lead in a good way. Like now."

"Yes, Miss. Thank you, Miss," said Tamara.

"I'll tell you what I'm going to do," said Mrs Cole. "Gideon, you and I will contact your leaders today. We have a staff meeting after school. If everyone agrees, we'll try to set up a video talk for one day this week. How does that sound?"

They all nodded and said, "Yes Miss. Thank you Miss," even Keren, which made everyone smile.

Then they were back out in the corridor and Tamara wanted to jump in the air and whoop with relief.

"Wow, Tam, you were awesome!" said Keren.

Tamara thought she would burst with pride. "If this works out, Dean and Lola will have to listen," she said.

And Yaz, she told herself. But she didn't feel very hopeful.

Gidi was patting her on the arm and grinning at her. He looked so much happier.

I have to harness my chilli temper for good, Tamara told herself, as they walked to class.

15

Pomegranates for Peace

"What time is the special assembly tomorrow morning, Tamara?" asked Mum at dinner on Tuesday evening.

Dad was home for once and said, "What's this?"

"The school's doing a video call with leaders from Gidi and Keren's club in Israel," said Mum. "There's been some tension in the school since October 7th. They thought it would be helpful to hear an Israeli Arab and Jew speak about peace."

The Head had announced the special assembly on Tuesday morning. Mrs Cole had managed to arrange everything with the teachers really quickly, as though they also felt something needed to be done urgently. Omer had messaged Gidi to say they were looking forward to talking to his classmates and Gidi was really excited about the assembly.

But Tamara felt more and more nervous about all the things that could go wrong.

And what about Dad?

"I have work tomorrow morning," he said now.

Tamara felt her chilli temper rise at Dad's tone. But then she thought about Mrs Cole's words.

Harness that power for good.

Here goes, she thought. "The assembly starts at nine o'clock," she said in a steady voice. "Mrs Cole said our families could come too."

Dad opened his mouth to speak, but she cut him off. "Becky's mum and dad are coming. You can sit with them."

Tamara fixed Dad with a cool stare.

Dad was holding his fork in mid-air and for a moment he froze.

Then looking down, he muttered, "I suppose I could go into work late."

Yesss! Tamara almost cried out.

Then Eden said, "I'm coming too."

"No, darling," said Mum. "But we'll start the paper chains tonight."

Gidi groaned and then he tickled Eden and they broke into laughter.

Tamara could hardly sleep that night for worry. What will Lola and Dean do? Will Yaz make an excuse and go off with Kadija? she wondered. What if the video freezes and everyone loses interest?

Then it was morning, and they were walking to school with Mum and Dad.

"Nervous?" said Keren, putting her arm through Tamara's.

"Very," said Tamara.

"Don't worry," said Keren. "Look, you've done your best." She gave Tamara's arm a tense squeeze.

The grown-ups left them at the school gates and walked off.

Tamara and her cousins joined the rest of Year 7 in the hall with the teachers. The parents sat on chairs down the side and Tamara caught Dad's eye. She nodded and to her surprise, he gave her a thumbs up. I must be doing something right for once, she told herself and sat down in a row with Gidi, Keren, Arthur and Josh.

Dean and his mates were in the back row. Jermaine and Zak sat together in the front row and Selma was a few seats along. But to Tamara's annoyance, Lola and her mean-girl group, sat in the row behind her again. Lola glared at Tamara and mouthed, Is-rael. Tamara stuck her chin in the air and turned back.

She had to search the hall to see where Yaz was sitting and finally spotted her on the end of a row, looking rather alone – a closed, pinched look on her face. No Kadija, thought Tamara. She's in Year 9.

Then Yaz looked up and caught Tamara's eye and such a look of sadness and confusion crossed her face. Tamara's heart went out to her old friend, and she lifted her hand in a cautious gesture to say hi. Yaz raised her hand for a second and Tamara felt a warm glow spread through her. Maybe Yaz hasn't completed turned against me, she thought.

Mrs Cole motioned to everyone to be quiet and then she said, "We're very lucky today to have two speakers from Israel . . ."

A couple of loud snickers at the word *Israel*.

The Head glared and said, "Anyone who cannot behave will be removed and will see me after."

She stood glaring for another few seconds as if to make her point and then said, "Omer is an Israeli Jew and Farrah is an Israeli Arab and a Muslim. They both live in Haifa and work for an organisation called Pomegranates for Peace. This is a group that brings together Israeli Jewish and Muslim children. Gideon Cohen attends this group and so does his sister, Keren, who has joined us this week from Israel. I want you all to listen very carefully to everything Omer and Farrah have to say."

The Head nodded to the IT technician at the back and the huge screen over the stage crackled into life.

A young man and young woman appeared on the screen, smiling and nodding.

"That's Omer and Farrah," said Gidi in an excited whisper to Tamara.

"Great," said Tamara.

"Welcome to London," said the Head and the two on the screen nodded. "I would also like to welcome those parents who could join us today."

Tamara looked round at Mum and Dad. Mum was

smiling, Dad was staring at the screen.

"Over to you, Omer and Farrah," said the Head and she sat down.

Omer raised his hand, palm out and said, "Hello to you, Abbey Park High School. Please excuse my English. Not very good."

He nodded to Farrah. "Hi, students," she said in an American accent. "We're very happy to meet you today."

"You can see, Farrah speak good English," said Omer and the two grinned at each other.

Lola kicked the back of Tamara's chair and Tamara swivelled round.

Lola mouthed, *Sooo stupid!*

But instead of flaring up, Tamara pursed up her lips and shrugged. Then she turned back. I won't let her wind me up today, Tamara told herself.

"I am Israeli Arab and Muslim," Farrah was saying. "My family lives in Haifa. My father works in the hospital. We always had Jewish friends and Muslim friends and Christian friends. I grew up in a family that believes that everyone in Israel can live together and work for peace. We want to stop all this war and hatred against each other. Omer is my friend."

Omer nodded. "I was born in Israel. My grandfather come from Germany to escape Nazis who kill so many Jews. But I want to make peace not war. In our club we bring kids together from Jewish and Muslim homes. They see everyone the same, normal, just like them. They make friends, play together, do lots of things together. It is very hard time in Israel and Gaza now. All the peoples suffering. Farrah has family in Gaza and she is very scared for them. Come, Yussuf." Omer pulled a boy in front of the screen.

The boy grinned and called out, "Shalom, Gidi."

Everyone turned to look at Gidi who called out, "Shalom, Yussuf."

Farrah said, "This is Yussuf. He plays chess with Gidi in our club. They speak Hebrew because Gidi doesn't speak Arabic and Yussuf doesn't speak English. Why are you friends, Yussuf?" Farrah asked the boy.

Tamara stared at Yussuf who was no taller than Gidi, but very dark with almost black hair, thicker than Gidi's and a cheeky grin on his face. I've never met an Arab boy before, she realised, and now I'm meeting Gidi's best friend. A comfortable feeling settled in her stomach as she listened to Yussuf speak Hebrew in a different accent. An Arabic accent? she wondered.

"I will translate," said Farrah. "Yussuf says, he lives three floors below Gidi. They love chess. Every week in our club they play chess and Yussuf says he always wins."

She laughed and Omer and Yussuf, along with many of the kids in the hall, also laughed.

"In our club, kids do what you do," said Omer, pointing towards the screen. "They play games, look at their phones together, listen to music, like you Abbey Park High, yes?"

"Yes," went up voices all around the hall.

Great, thought Tamara, exchanging looks with Keren.

"I say to kids in our club, this is what peace looks like and feels like. Muslim and Jew, sitting together, not fighting, not shouting, but good friends. This is peace. That is what we believe in for all Israelis and Palestinians."

A faint wail went up in the background and Omer stopped. He and Farrah exchanged nods.

"It is the siren," said Omer. "There is air raid. We must to go to bomb shelter, chaverim. Remember, you must to work for peace. Like Gidi and Yussuf. Help all children like you be safe and live without war. Shalom. Salaam."

Then the screen went blank and a silence fell over the hall.

No! thought Tamara. That wasn't enough!

All around her kids were picking up bags, talking about football and other things.

It was a waste of time, she thought, feeling her shoulders drop.

Even the Head and the teachers looked confused, as if they didn't know what to do now. Then to her shock, Gidi stood up and called out, "Yussuf and me went to the bomb shelter together on October 7th."

Everyone stopped and the Head motioned to them to sit down again.

Gidi waited for the hall to quieten down. Then he continued, "We were very scared. We thought we'd be killed. Everyone was scared – Yussuf's mum and dad, my mum and dad. I couldn't stop being scared. That's why . . ." He paused and stared down at his sister, who gave him a nod. "That's why I line up my pencils," Gidi said in a rush. "It helps me to keep calm when I'm worried. In your school, I'm often worried. When kids make you choose sides, Israel or Palestine, I feel scared again, like in the bomb shelter. Me and Yussuf don't take sides. Maybe you don't know but I can tell you, all the kids in Israel are scared terrorists will come and kidnap them, hide them away in tunnels in Gaza."

A gasp went up around the hall and people started talking.

"Quiet!" called out the Head. "Go on, Gideon."

"All the kids are scared in Israel – Muslims, Jews, Bedouin, Druze, Christians, all kids – because the terrorists attacked everyone on October 7th, not just Jews. And my abba – um, dad – says it's the same in Gaza. All the kids are terrified in Gaza because their homes are bombed and their families killed." He stopped for a moment to catch his breath but to Tamara's relief there was silence in the hall.

They're listening. Finally! she thought.

Gidi started again. "I'm for peace, not hate and war. Some people in your school have been nasty to me because I'm from Israel."

"Free Palestine!" came a voice from the back.

A teacher stood up, went to the back row and gave the boy a warning.

Tamara swivelled round and caught Dean's eye. To her surprise, he raised his eyebrows and gave her a slight nod. Maybe Dean is ready for peace too, she thought.

Then she tried to catch Yaz's eye but Yaz was staring into space.

Is she even listening? wondered Tamara, feeling the sadness rise again, but Gidi was still speaking.

"But most people have been very friendly," he said, and Selma swivelled round and gave him an encouraging nod. "So now I have friends from many different countries. You have a lot of different kids in London." Gidi gave a cautious grin and a couple of people laughed back.

Then he said, "Pakistan."

Whoops around the hall.

"Poland."

More whoops.

"Jamaica."

Jermaine and Zak did a high five.

"Thailand."

Arthur threw up his ball and caught it as a teacher, stood up, glared at him and then sat down again.

"And loads more I don't even know," Gidi went on. "But Omer and Farrah say it doesn't matter where you come from, it's what you say and what you do that makes a difference. I don't care where you come from. I just like to hang up."

The hall erupted as people shouted back, "HANG OUT!"

Gidi stood there grinning and Tamara thought she'd never seen him look so confident.

Gidi remained standing as the hall began to quieten down. But suddenly a ball of paper wrapped around something solid, flew through the air straight at Gidi's head.

Lola called out in a mocking voice, "Duck, Israel, it's a bomb."

Too late! The missile hit Gidi's cheek. His hand flew up and when he dropped it, Tamara could see a red mark on the skin.

"Gidi!" she cried out.

Teachers grabbed Lola and pulled her out as the girl protested, "What! He said stuff. Why can't I say stuff? He should stop killing babies in Gaza."

But the teachers marched her out of the hall.

The Head was standing on the stage, not speaking, as if she'd lost her nerve.

This is crazy, thought Tamara and she threw herself to her feet as the heat of her chilli temper threatened to explode. All eyes were on her. She could feel the heat of their stares.

I can't just stand here, Tamara told herself. I have to harness my chilli power and say something. She opened her mouth but her voice was not much above a whisper, she was so nervous. "When my dad told me Gidi was coming to stay . . ."

"Speak up!" someone shouted.

Tamara took a breath and went on in a stronger voice. "We had a terrible row. It was all my fault. I had to move out of my bedroom and share with my little sister and I didn't want to. I was so selfish and Dad told me so. Gidi and all our family in Israel have had a terrible time since October 7th. I'm so sorry, Gidi."

Tamara stopped.

Gidi's raised his head and did a thumbs up.

Tamara grinned and said, "Gidi is amazing. He's so brave and he's a good friend to everyone and he's mega clever."

"Brilliant at CHESS!!" roared out Selma in such a huge voice everyone laughed for a few seconds.

But then they all went silent again as if willing Tamara to go on.

"Gidi knows about peace," said Tamara. "He's been telling me and my friends since he got here, only I wouldn't listen and neither would some other people . . ."

Her voice faltered and she stared towards Yaz.

To her surprise, Yaz wiped a hand across her eyes.

Tamara went on, "I wanted to fight everyone who insulted us Jewish kids and called us Is-rael as though that was a rude word." She looked around the room. Some people wouldn't meet her eye and others shot her mocking grins. They won't stop me, Tamara told herself.

"Gidi's lived through a war," she went on. "But he doesn't say to people, Are you Israel or Palestine? He doesn't say nasty things about Palestinians because he's Israeli. Gidi says his club, Pomegranates for Peace, and all the dozens of peace groups in Israel, are building a bridge between their communities to bring people together and work for peace."

Many eyes were looking at her now, listening.

"We should do that in our school," Tamara went on. "Build bridges, not take sides and shout at each other. I've decided I'm going to speak up for peace *every* day from now on."

There was silence for a moment and then Jermaine and Zak in the front row stood up, turned towards Tamara and started clapping. Selma joined them and then clapping started to spread all around the hall. The Head was nodding towards Tamara from the stage and the teachers gave approving nods too. When Tamara looked around, Dean was clapping too. He stopped when he caught her eye but then he gave her a brief nod. She nodded back.

You can change some people's minds, Tamara thought. But Lola might be a bigger problem. She couldn't see Yaz and then the Head told everyone to sit down and be quiet.

"Well done to Gidi and Tamara," said the Head, "and many thanks to Omer, Farrah and Yussuf. I will be in touch with them later today. For now, there is a lot to think about. Maybe you can make time in your lessons this morning to talk with your teachers. Today has helped our school to open the discussion about the war between Israel and Gaza and what each one of us can do to build peace. We will be following it up with more assemblies in the future. As I said last week, this is a school built on friendship, no matter where you or your families come from. Everyone is welcome at Abbey Park High. Teachers, dismiss your classes."

Everyone moved off, chattering and swinging their bags. Some people called out to Gidi, "See you later, mate."

"*Yoffee Toffee.*"

"Bet you beat that Yussuf kid at chess sometimes."

That made Gidi laugh as he walked off with Arthur and Josh.

"Coming, Tam?" said Keren.

"Give me a sec," said Tamara. She was searching the hall for Yaz.

The others went off and then she felt a cool hand on her arm. Looking round she saw her friend, her eyes wide, staring at her.

"You were brilliant," said Yaz in a shaky voice. "You and Gidi and Omer and Farrah. I'm so sorry, Tam. I didn't listen. I let Kadija get inside my head and she and her crowd, they don't have any space for peace. They can only see one side in this horrible war and it makes them, well, quite racist sometimes. That's not me, Tam, you know I'm not racist."

"OK," said Tamara, although she still felt uncertain. "But what will Kadija say?"

"I don't care anymore," declared Yaz in a stronger voice.

Tamara nodded and there was a pause. Then she said, "I've missed you."

"Me too!" said Yaz in such a strong voice they both grinned. "We can work for peace together, Tam. I'm ready. What's the plan?"

Tamara felt that warm glow return as she drank in her old friend's words. Yaz was sincere, she really meant it, Tamara was certain.

Then she had a thought.

"OK," she said. "How about we start a club for peace in the school. I don't know yet what we'd do . . ."

"Great idea. We could have a sleepover this weekend, make a list. Meanwhile I'll Google all the peace organisations in Israel and see if any of them meet in London. We could invite them over to speak at our school," said Yaz, a concentrated frown on her face.

She sounds just like the old Yaz, Tamara thought, and she flung her arms around her friend. They hugged for what seemed ages.

When they pulled apart, Yaz said, "Better get to class."

But Tamara had spotted Dad standing on his own.

Mum had walked off with Becky's dad. He looked over at her as if he was waiting for her. Butterflies filled her tummy again. Better get it over with, she told herself.

"I'll be along in a minute," said Tamara and Yaz slung her school bag over her shoulder and walked off.

The hall had emptied and was very quiet as Tamara walked over to her father, heart thumping.

But to her surprise her father put his hands on her shoulders and bent his face down so that their foreheads were almost touching.

"I'm so sorry, my darling Tam," Dad said in a low voice. "I was so upset after October 7th and so scared your uncle David, my little brother, would be killed in the war, I took it out on you. I was so unfair to you."

He stopped and they stared into each other's eyes.

Tamara felt relief spread through her.

Dad doesn't hate me, she told herself. Gran told me he was taking his fear out on me and she was right. I needed to be more patient. Not get so angry all the time.

"S'OK, Dad," she said.

"No," said Dad. "It's not, but thank you, my sweet girl. And I'm so proud of the way you've looked after Gidi. I didn't realise what a terrible time you've been having at school. Mum says the video call with Omer and Farrah was your idea. That was utterly brilliant, Tam. And I couldn't believe how you stood up today and spoke out. Everyone listened to you. You're a real leader, Tam. I'm so proud of you."

Tamara stood there, basking in the warmth of his voice and the comfortable pressure of his hands on her shoulders.

Then a thought came to her.

"When we were at the top of the Shard, Dad, were you scared to look out of those huge windows, like me?"

"Course," he said, with a grin. "I've always been terrified of heights. We're the same, you and me, Tam. And I've got a bit of a chilli temper too, ask your mum."

That was a surprise.

Then Dad went off to work and Tamara went to join the others for lessons.

16

First Night Chanukah — December 7th, 2023

The rest of Wednesday was quite strange at school, with some people talking about everything that had been said and others not really interested. Tamara didn't want to join in with any more heavy talks about war and stuff. Gidi and Keren seemed to feel the same.

As they all walked home after the last lesson, Gidi, said, "I'm staying on the sofa, cousin, even when Keren goes. You should have your room back."

"Eden will be offended if I don't share with her," said Tamara.

"I'll make her a trillion bracelets," said Gidi.

"You sound like a proper English boy these days," said Arthur, and he raced off to catch up with Josh.

"He's my mate," said Gidi in a low voice.

"You're proper mates," said Tamara and they laughed.

Sitting in the living room that evening after dinner, Mum said, "Your dad and I have decided you all deserve a party on Thursday night for first night of Chanukah. Invite your friends. Just let me know numbers."

"Yess!" cried out Gidi and Tamara together, bumping fists.

"Yaz, Becky, Hannah," said Tamara.

"Yaz?" interrupted Mum. "You're friends again."

Tamara just gave a brief nod.

"Arthur and Josh," went on Gidi.

"Zak and Jermaine . . ."

" . . . and Selma."

"OK," said Tamara, "but no chess."

Then Eden lifted a huge box of chocolates off the sideboard and said, "Can we open these now, please, Mummy, please. I need it."

"I was saving those for Chanukah," complained Mum, with a frown.

"Nah," said Dad, grinning. "Eden's right. We absolutely need those now."

Everyone cheered and Dad pulled off the plastic wrapper and passed the box around.

Me and Dad, thought Tamara, as she ate a coffee cream, her favourite – we're the same. He said so. It felt so good, she even let Eden have the other coffee cream. Nothing could burst her bubble tonight.

Tamara spent the rest of the evening messaging everyone about the Chanukah party.

Her first message was to Yaz.

chanukah party ours tomorrow after school

Her finger hovered over Send for ages. What if she says no? Or she's with Kadija? But in the end Tamara decided she just had to go for it and pressed the button.

Two seconds later her phone bleeped.

squeeeee . . . cant wait xxxxxxxxxxxxxxxxxxxx

Tamara gave a sigh of relief and messaged the others. The last message was to Jermaine. She'd already checked with Mum and Dad.

will baz let me have one of his kittens present for Eden.

There was a pause. He's checking with Baz, Tamara thought.

Then Jermaine was typing.

baz says OK bring it tomorrow

Tamara was so excited it took her ages to fall asleep.

The next day was Thursday and Gidi, Keren and Tamara sat with all their friends in the lunchroom, chatting about the Chanukah party that evening,

"So, what is Chanukah?" asked Jermaine.

"When the Jews defeated the Greeks," said Josh.

"They were led by Judah Maccabee," put in Tamara. "The Maccabees won and took back their country but the Greeks had smashed up the Temple in Jerusalem. There wasn't enough oil to keep the eternal light burning and it would take eight days to get more. But a miracle happened. The lights kept burning for eight days . . ."

" . . . so we celebrate by lighting candles for eight nights and getting presents every night," finished Becky with a grin.

"Wow," said Jermaine. "We only get presents on Christmas Day."

As Tamara walked to afternoon classes with Yaz, Gidi and Keren, she saw Dean up ahead. He caught her eye and stopped.

What now? she thought, feeling tense.

But Dean gave Gidi a nod and said, "Your club in Israel sounds OK, mate." Then he strolled off, hands in his pockets.

A broad grin spread across Gidi's face. He and Tamara high-fived.

"Unbelievable," said Tamara, grinning round at the others.

Yaz had ducked her head and now she looked up and met Tamara's eyes.

Tamara nodded.

We don't need to say anything, she thought. We both know Yaz went off with Kadija for a while and things were horrid between us. But Yaz isn't Dean. She definitely isn't Lola, Tamara told herself. Me and Yaz, we're solid again. Just like always.

Gidi and Keren had walked on.

But Tamara made a fist and she and Yaz had a gentle bump. Then they caught up with the others and were chatting away when a familiar voice sounded behind them.

"That was a load of rubbish all that peace stuff, Is-rael."

Tamara swivelled on her heel, as Yaz reached out a calming hand. It was Lola and the mean girls, striding arm in arm, filling the corridor.

No! thought Tamara. Not this time. Drawing herself up to her full height, she met Lola square on and said in a mocking voice, "Who cares what you think, Lola *Ethel* Pantry."

"*Ethel!!*" shrieked one of the mean girls. "That's my great aunty's name. You serious?! You're so last century, Lola!"

Tamara watched as a fuming Lola, silenced at last, walked off behind the other girls, still shrieking and calling out *E-thel!* to each other.

"How did you know her middle name?" said Yaz, grinning.

"Overheard a teacher say it. Lola went mad, saying she hated it and didn't want anyone to know," said Tamara. "I was saving it up for the right moment."

"Great timing, Cousin," said Keren and they walked on, calling out Ethel between them. Warrior Gran will be so proud of me, Tamara told herself as she took her seat in class. I didn't get chilli mad. I kept my cool but I still hit the bullseye. With words, not fists.

The day flew by and then it was Thursday evening and the Chanukah party.

Eden and Gidi had made a huge pile of paper chains

the night before. Dad was home early and helped to decorate the living room.

Gran arrived with her own Chanukiah. "It's first night, so we only light the shamash and one candle," she told them. "That's two Chanukiahs, with yours."

"Three," said Becky, who'd arrived earlier. She pulled a small Chanukiah out of a bag. "Mum said I should bring it."

"We going to light loads of candles," said Eden in a contented voice.

The doorbell went and Tamara heard Jermaine's voice. She rushed down the hall and put her finger to her lips. Jermaine pulled a tiny ginger kitten out of his coat.

"She's beautiful," whispered Tamara. She ran upstairs to bring down a cardboard box she'd hidden in Mum and Dad's bedroom. Inside Tamara had made a soft bed and there were holes in the lid.

Back downstairs they settled the kitten in the box.

"We'll put it on this little table and then you come and get it after we light the candles." Jermaine nodded, with a grin.

By five o'clock, when it was dark outside, everyone had arrived.

Becky and Hannah stood together near Becky's Chanukiah, ready to light up.

Eden stood with Mum, who had put out two extra candles for the hostages, like small tealights. Tamara linked arms with Yaz and they stood near Gran.

Jermaine, Arthur, Josh, Selma, Hannah, Gidi and Keren, stood around in a semi-circle.

Then Dad stepped up to speak.

"Tonight we light the Chanukah candles like Jews all over the world will do and have done since Judah and the Maccabees defeated the Greeks, more than two thousand years ago. To all of you who haven't celebrated Chanukah before . . ."

Jermaine gave a nod. Selma exchanged looks with Gidi. Arthur shrugged.

Arthur knows all about it, thought Tamara. Like Yaz. They always come over one of the nights.

" . . . welcome to our celebration," Dad went on with a warm smile. "Chanukah recalls how the Greeks ransacked the Temple in Jerusalem. Judah and his Maccabees fought the Greeks and won. They took back Jerusalem and rededicated the Temple.

He paused for a moment and then he said, "This is the first Jewish festival since the terrible attacks in Israel on October 7th – the worst attack on the Jewish people since the Holocaust."

Everyone looked very solemn as his words sank in.

Yaz gave Tamara's arm a squeeze.

"A lot has happened since October 7th and a terrible war is raging," Dad said. "Peace and the release of all the hostages seems far away. But like Gidi's club in Israel, as Omer said on Tuesday, this is what peace looks like and feels like. I'm very proud to be with you all tonight."

Yes, thought Tamara, looking around. Yaz and Selma from Muslim families, Arthur from Thailand, Jermaine whose grandparents were born in Jamaica, together with all our Jewish friends and family.

Then Selma said, with a puzzled frown, "If it's the first night, why are there two candles in each ... er..."

"Chanukiah," said Eden, looking pleased with herself.

"Good question," said Dad. "The candle in the middle is called the shamash, or servant candle. We light that first each night and then we light the other candles with it. We don't strike another match."

Selma gave an approving nod.

Dad looked over at Mum and Mum struck a match. She lit the two small tealights. "These are to remember the hostages in Gaza," she said. Then she lit the shamash on their family Chanukiah and said, "Keren, light the candle for the first night."

Tamara felt a swell of pride that Keren, the eldest cousin, was called up to light.

Becky lit her shamash and Hannah lit the first candle.

Then Gran said, "Jermaine, would you light my shamash?"

Jermaine stepped up and lit the candle, then he pulled it out of the candle holder and turned and offered the candle to Arthur.

"Not me," said Arthur. "Gidi should do it."

"You do it, mate," said Gidi in his best London voice.

A giggle washed around the room and then Arthur, looking very serious, took the shamash from Jermaine and lit the candle.

They all stood for a moment and then Mum led the prayer, finishing ". . . verzi vonu, shel Chanukah."

After chorusing, "Amen", the Jewish family and friends, with Eden jumping up and down, sang the first verse of the traditional Chanukah song, 'Ma Oztur'.

The song seemed to release a seriousness in the room and everyone started to talk in loud voices until Mum clapped her hands and called out, "Now, it's presents."

"Sorry, Mrs Cohen, I didn't bring anything," said Jermaine, looking anxious.

But Mum laughed and said, "Of course not, darling, we have presents for you."

She pulled out a huge bag from behind the sofa and began to hand round wrapped parcels to everyone. Meanwhile, Tamara had nodded to Jermaine who sneaked out into the hall and returned with the box.

Eden spotted it first and called out, "What's that?"

"It's a present for you," said Jermaine with a grin. "From your sister."

Eden bounced up and down on her toes, clapping her hands as Jermaine put the box down on a chair.

"Can I open it now, Tamsy?" cried out Eden.

"Go for it!" said Tamara with a laugh.

Everyone stood round as the little girl removed the lid.

Tamara thought she would never forget the look on her sister's face and the delighted squeal as Eden put her hands in the box and picked up the little kitten. Hugging it to her chest, she said, "It's the best present I've ever had."

Hannah and Becky gathered round to stroke the kitten.

Tamara had stood back for a moment and then Gidi came over to her side.

"Maybe she'll stop sucking her thumb now," he said in a quiet voice.

"Dunno," said Tamara with a shrug.

"Not very hygienic if you've got a pet," said Gidi. He paused and then he said, "Maybe I can stop lining up my pencils."

Tamara stared over at her cousin, the boy who'd come into her life despite her mean thoughts. Something her father had said earlier that day, came into her mind.

"Dad says in every generation a hero like Judah the Maccabee rises up to lead the Jewish people. I vote for you."

"Doesn't have to be a man," said Gidi. "I vote for you."

Tamara nodded and said, "I suppose we've both got a big job then."

The floor was littered with wrapping paper. People

were looking at each other's presents. Mum was handing round donuts and potato latkes and the table was groaning with more food.

Is this my most important Chanukah? wondered Tamara. When Gidi came I thought my life would change forever, giving up my bedroom to a boy. That seems very stupid and babyish now. The truth is, she told herself, Gidi *has* changed my life forever. He's shown me that I don't have to fight with my fists and my chilli temper against racism and hatred. I have to work for peace and help to change the world. Like Gidi and Yussuf do in their club in Israel.

Gran had said at Friday night dinner last week, "The war won't go on forever. We have to decide what the peace will look like."

Now Tamara told herself, peace will come but until it does, I'm going work for peace, however long it takes.

Author's Note

This has been the most challenging book I have written, out of ten published novels, short stories, poems and song lyrics. I began the book six months after October 7th 2023 and finished writing in January 2025 while the Israel /Gaza war was still raging. My hope is that the hostages will be released and a ceasefire will take place before my book is published.

The work to create and maintain a lasting peace in the Middle East will take a long time after all the death and destruction on both sides. I hope that in some small way my book will contribute towards Peace Building between Israelis and Palestinians.

I want to thank my publisher, Elaine Bousfield, founder and director of Zuntold Books, who suggested in April 2024 that I write a book post-October 7th for young people. I was very uncertain at first but then I decided that my book would have peace at its heart and the writing engine turned on.

My husband Rafael, who always speaks up for peace, has supported this book from the first ideas. My grandson, Jacob, at ten years old, read the whole book and made many good suggestions, including helping to shape the title. My good friend, award-winning author, Penny Joelson, has also been very influential in helping to guide the journey of my story.

In Israel our nephew Ittay Flescher, director of Kids4Peace, bringing Israeli and Palestinian teens together in Jerusalem, has provided important background information. I am grateful to Jane Krivine of the Freddy Krivine Initiative for feedback from Israeli Jewish and Arab children. Mohammad Fahili, director of the Clore Jewish-Arab Community Centre, Akko, Israel and Clare King Lassman have provided very important input for my research and encouraged Israeli Arab teens to complete my questionnaire.

My huge thank you to all the young people in the UK and Israel, from a variety of backgrounds, who have spoken to me and completed written questionnaires, with their thoughts and feelings after October 7th 2023. They have shared with such openness, honesty and with great maturity and they give me real cause for hope that they will be the future Peace Builders.

I have put some examples of their comments below. All respondents are anonymous.

After October 7th if you're looking at a recipe on social media, for example, in the comments it's things like Free Palestine, why aren't you talking about Palestine, on and on down the screen. I mean, why under a recipe?
Jewish girl, 13 years, London, UK

On social media I see negative rhetoric like all Palestinians are bombers and terrorists. On the flip side I see similar remarks for Jews. While there may be some sort of positive trait people place on both sides, the negatives have pushed far stronger in my perspective.
Israeli Arab Muslim boy, 15 years, Haifa, Israel

No-one talks about the hostages or atrocities of October 7th unless they have some connection to Israel or Judaism when actually we all have a connection because we are all human beings and this could as easily have happened to us or someone we knew.
Jewish girl, 13 years, London, UK

I have never met a Jew before and you discovered that the (Jewish) children have no problem playing and talking with us.
Israeli Arab Muslim girl, 10 years, Freddy Krivine summer camp for Israeli Jews and Arabs

I learnt that they [the Arab children] are not violent at all.
Israeli Jewish boy, 10 years, Freddy Krivine summer camp

I feel disappointed in humanity and feel like humans have lost their feelings of empathy when I see comments from people on both sides that express extreme views on the ongoing war. I have heard and seen many people that think when a tragedy occurs to the other side, that it is a victory. They perceive it as a great achievement instead of wishing for peace and all this to end as soon as possible.
Israeli Arab Muslim boy, 14 years, Haifa, Israel

I was born in Israel and lived there until I was five. We have a lot of family affected by the attack. Last holiday my parents said we would go to Israel. They told us that we may have to go down on the floor in the car if there is a bomb. Luckily it didn't happen but for that whole conversation I was crying at the thought of being in danger of a bomb hitting me. It was one of the most scary things I've ever dealt with.
Jewish girl, 13 years, Israel and London, UK

If I want to talk about the ongoing situation I talk with my roommate in school. He is Jewish. He doesn't share the same opinions as me but he is very respectful. He understands me and tries to explain the Jewish perspective of the war. It helps when I talk to him and he acknowledges my feelings. We talk about the war weekly and I feel relieved while talking to him. I see the hope that is still here – two boys, one Muslim and one Jewish, living together peacefully and talking about topics that even politicians couldn't talk about without shouting.

Israeli Arab Muslim boy, 15 years, Haifa, Israel

I'm in a cricket club and I'm the only Jewish boy. I know the other boys are pro-Palestinian but it doesn't matter. We all just play cricket as a team.

Jewish boy, 13 years, London, UK

All the incidents of racism in this book are based on my own personal experience as a British Jewish citizen and on experiences reported to me by Jewish young people and adults, by Muslim friends and by black students when I was a teacher. I have also taken incidents reported in the media, including social media.

Ultimately my book asks, What can each person do for

peace? Here is my Toolbox of ideas to help readers start on their own journeys as Peace Builders.

1: Read a good book

Books can change lives. Fiction inspires and a good book could be your route map to peace. In her famous diary Anne Frank said, "How wonderful it is that nobody need wait a single moment before starting to improve the world."

Here are a few book recommendations:

After Tomorrow by Gillian Cross
The total breakdown of UK society forces everyone to head for France but the French are overwhelmed by British refugees and close the Channel Tunnel. Flipping the Calais migrant problem on its head, Gillian Cross forces us to think: if we Brits had to flee, who would tolerate us and let us in?

Red Leaves by Sita Brahmachari
Brings together a Somali refugee, a boy whose mum is a journalist in Syria, a homeless girl and an ancient elder. The book explores the struggles young people face to negotiate peace in a troubled world.

Hidden by Miriam Halahmy (yes, that's me)
My novel focuses on human rights and tolerance. What would you do if your friend begged you to hide an asylum seeker to save them from being deported? Alix has never thought about immigration before but faced with a huge dilemma, she learns how to stand up for what she believes in and how to influence those around her.

Saving Rafael by Leslie Wilson
A Christian family saves a Jewish boy in Nazi Berlin.

Boy Overboard by Morris Gleitzman
A hilarious book on football, asylum seekers, war and survival.

Infinite Sky by CJ Flood
What if travellers camped at the end of your garden?

Looking at the Stars by Jo Cotterill
Brother and sister made refugees from their country by 'peace-keeping' troops.

2: Make a video

YouTube is the second biggest search engine on the planet. If you want to speak up for peace, get together with friends and make a video. Take a look at my video for peace on YouTube: https://www.youtube.com/watch?v=w4f-TXnQOJE

3: Do nothing!

Bit weird, I know. But sometimes we see intolerance in school or on the streets and don't know how to react. In my book, *Hidden*, the main character, Alix, sees the "foreign boy" Samir suffering racist bullying on the street. She speaks out for him and the gang turn on her. But was that the safest thing to do? Alix could have been badly hurt. In this situation I would recommend standing back, but don't snigger or the victim will feel worse. Do nothing – but don't just walk away. Go up to the victim afterwards and support them, make sure they don't feel alone anymore.

4: Write a poem

We know how inspiring the written word can be. So why not write something yourself about peace and tolerance? You could read it out to your friends and family, enter a poetry competition or publish in the school magazine. John Lennon wrote, "If everyone demanded peace instead of another TV set, then there'd be peace."

Make your words count.

5: Rap for peace

Music and lyrics have always been tools for change.

In one of my poems, Light a Candle, I write, "Light a candle/ light another one/ light seven billion candles for peace."

My poem has been set to music and sung by school choirs in the UK.

Check out this video of two Kenyan boys who rap for peace: https://www.youtube.com/watch?v=gQ0QWOdCPfc&t=3s

6: Support the Peace Builders

There are so many wonderful peace groups which are working to build peace in the Middle East. You can find out more about them at ALLMEP: the Alliance for Middle East Peace: https://www.allmep.org/

Choose one peace organisation and start a peace group in school to learn about their work and support them.

7: Books not Bullets

"Books not bullets will pave the path towards peace and prosperity." This is a message to world leaders from Nobel Prize winner, Malala Yousafzai on her 18th birthday. Read her inspiring memoir, *I am Malala: The Girl Who Stood Up For Education*. You could hold a Malala-readathon in your school and raise money for a peace organisation.

8: Last thoughts

It is easy to sit at home and moan about war

and intolerance, or complain about conflict in the playground and on our streets. But you can make up your mind to speak up for peace from now on.

Dip into my toolbox to get started and good luck.
Shalom/Salaam/Peace.

Miriam Halahmy
London,
January 2025

'Truly gripping.'
Saffia Farr, Editor, JUNO Magazine

'A must-read of our times.'
WRD Magazine

'A heart-stopping portrayal. Essential reading for teens and parents of teens – this book may well save lives.'
Angela Kiverstein

'A crucial read – current and compelling.'
Penny Joelson

'Poignant, powerful and educational.'
*Emma Suffield,
SLA UK School Librarian of the Year 2018*

'Impossible to put down.'
Lucas Maxwell, Portable Magic Dispenser

'A very important book.'
From Bee With Love

Nominated for the Carnegie Medal

ALWAYS
HERE FOR YOU

14-year-old Holly is lonely.
Her parents are never around after Gran's Crisis, and best friend Amy has moved across the Atlantic to Canada. Home alone with no-one to talk to, Holly is at rock bottom. That is, until she finds Jay.

Caring, funny and with so much in common her, Jay is the perfect guy – they talk online, but Holly knows to be careful, she's heard the horror stories.

As they grow closer and closer, chatting with Jay is all that makes Holly happy. But as Holly lets her guard down, is Jay everything he seems?
Is Holly in too deep? And is it too late?

Always Here For You is an unforgettable novel from acclaimed poet, novelist and special needs educator, Miriam Halahmy.

For more insightful books you will love,
and to take part in our Living Books
and Storyteller community,
head to

zuntold.com